The Amaretto

D.D. Corbitt

Copyright 2014 by D.D. Corbitt
Edited by Kelly Hartigan
Formatted by Polgarus Studio
Published by © D.D. Corbitt
Cover Design © Elle J. Rossi

ISBN: 978-0-9863289-1-6

Dedicated with love to my family: my mom and dad, Teresa and Duane Peil; Vernon Corbitt; and Chris Coppola … I miss you all; Dr. Wayne M. Eberle and Amy Eberle; my sister, Diane Rinaldi, and her family; and my biggest cheerleader and harshest critic, Michelle Rinaldi Ortega and her daughter Tori.

ACKNOWLEDGMENTS

A heartfelt Thank you to those who helped make my book become a reality.

Kelly Hartigan of XterraWeb for her expert editing and feedback.
http://editing.xterraweb.com

Elle J. Rossi. Of EJR Digital Art for the remarkable design and artwork
http://www.ejrdigitalart.com

and my Swamp Sister Pam Stack for her patience, guidance, laughter and memories of the Everglades.

Prologue – Present Day

It's so damned cold in here and the smells assault my senses. The odors are a cacophony of flowers, formaldehyde and all types of perfumes and colognes. I sit in the back of the "Peace" room because I couldn't find the "dance" room or the "it's been a hell of a ride" room. I am sad to be sending off an old friend. I am going to miss her terribly. Now, I have to contend with her grieving husband and my best friend, Randy.

It seemed only yesterday we had an adventure to end all adventures.

Randy looks over his shoulder to me and gives me his best "I'm pissed" look. He nods his head in the direction of the box at the head of the room. I can't figure out if he is asking me to come up there or he is saying, "I wish you were in the box and not Sue." I'm pretty sure it's the former, but who the hell can tell these days.

Ever since Sue was diagnosed with inoperable lung cancer, he has been on a roller coaster of emotion. And, through it all, I have been there, as always. Together, we have seen too much: too much pain, too much craziness, and too much of each other.

People mill around in little groups and speak in hushed voices saying the same old funeral clichés: "She looks so peaceful," "she looks like she is sleeping," and "they did a fantastic job," ad nauseum.

To me, Sue looks like a painted dead body in a box. She is dressed in clothes I don't think she would ever wear, and I wonder if some sick bastard put stiletto heels on her feet. I remind myself to peek, if and when, I get up there.

"Who the fuck are these people?" I ask myself as I scan the room.

Sue and I had known each other twenty-five years or so, and I never knew she had known so many people.

Once again, Randy catches my eyes. I sigh deeply and pry myself out of the brocade wing chair to sit next to him on the cold, hard wooden bench. He grabs my hand and looks at me like he is going to burst into tears at any moment. I feel sad for him.

I try not to look at the box with Sue's elevated head rising above the edge in a contorted kind of way.

"Please, stay here with me," Randy begs. "I can't get through this without you."

"Who are these people?" I can't help myself.

"Mostly her family and people she grew up with. Most of them I don't know. How long have we been married?"

"Which time?"

Randy had a nasty habit of collecting wives. He claimed he loved being married, but none ever lasted. He married Sue twice. I think he had six or seven ex-wives. I lost count years ago.

"Please, not now," he retorted.

"All together, about 30 years, maybe?" I ask more than answer. She was, by far, his favorite.

Sue's family and friends began pointing and whispering at me and Randy sitting together, holding hands. Finally, Sue's older sister, Debbie, approaches us and sits next to me.

"They have no idea that you both have been friends forever," she musters in a comforting sort of way, "I really feel bad for you both. I know she loved you very much. I think you were more of a sister to her than I was."

"It had to do with logistics. I just lived closer to her," I said trying to reassure her.

"I keep telling everyone that you were 'best person' at the weddings because of how long you and Randy have been friends," Debbie offers.

I'm thinking the eulogy is going to be very difficult. I have to not only say goodbye to my friend, but also justify my relationship with her husband. I think I'm going to be sick.

"Do you think you can handle this alone for a while?" I ask Randy. I need to get out of here. The stench is overwhelming, and I can feel a major headache coming on. I want nothing more than to go to *The Hole* or to Amaretto.

"Yeah. Go home. You don't look so good."

No kinder words were ever spoken.

I get up, bend over to give my friend a kiss on the cheek, and start toward the door. I pay no attention to anyone else and ease out to the parking lot.

Halfway home, I pull to the roadside, open the door, and spill my guts on the pavement. It doesn't make me feel better. I gingerly wipe my mouth on the only available cloth— my sleeve—and continue driving. The sun has already started sinking, and I know this won't go on much longer. Randy is going to have a house full of people, so I know my work is cut out for me. I offered the spare room in *The Hole* to ease the crowding, and since we live next door to each other on the same property, everyone can stay together. Hell, they can have the whole damned house and I will just sleep in my van. At this point, I don't really give a shit.

As I turn onto the unpaved, long winding driveway that leads to *The Hole*, I begin to realize that so much has changed since

Randy, Sue, and I scattered Pudge's ashes off the stern of Amaretto. It was, without a doubt, the most incredible journey we had ever taken. All those dead people ...

Since then, we all survived Hurricane Andrew, although our homes did not. My Mom died suddenly; my son, Shane, moved to the mountains and finally, *finally*, found a normal wife. I didn't see him much anymore, but with the cell phone and internet explosion, we were able to keep in touch. My constant companion, Mickey Dog, crossed the Rainbow Bridge and went through eternity's doggie door. His departure took a piece of my heart.

I think I may have fallen in love again despite insurmountable odds, but all love stories end tragically —at least mine do. But they leave me with fond memories and a smile. I am not the easiest person to get along with, and most times, even I can't stand living with me. And I am grateful to anyone who can convince me that I am worthy of love.

As I parked and stepped into the serenity of the evening, I suddenly felt all the energy drain from my body. If I looked down, I was sure it would all be a puddle around my feet. I drug my lead-laden legs into the house, kicked off my shoes, and headed to the inner sanctum of my room. I easily slipped out of my clothes, donned a T-shirt, and fell back onto my bed. I grabbed the golden anchor pendant I always wore and started to easily doze into a long passed lifetime.

Chapter 1 – Ten Years Earlier

Friends, Rum, Three Deaths, and The Secret

It wasn't an unusual day. At least it didn't start out that way. The best I can remember, I woke to the nagging knock at the door. It was the kind of knock that brings bad news. It's funny how knocks have personalities. No, this knock wasn't a hello knock or an I'm-glad-to-see-you knock or even an it's-been-a-long-time knock. This knock contained the irritating sting of an I'm-going-to-save-your-soul knock or a we-are-real-sorry-to-inform-you-that-so-and-so-has-died knock. Amid the scattered books and clothing on the floor, I found a wrap and managed to get it on by the time the knocking person had successfully completed a fourth gnawing and unnerving repetition of pounding. When I looked out the peephole, there was an official-looking man of about twenty-four years standing in the late morning sun, his USPS vehicle parked in the street.

"What is it?" I asked.

"Certified letter for Sandra Darnell," the voice answered.

Certified letter, I thought, who could be sending me one? The only people I know that send certified letters are certifiable members of the Internal Revenue Service, or some other government agency, warning people of impending financial doom. Everybody knows where I live—I have been here for more years than I can count—but this was almost *intriguing*. I opened the door a little— this is Dade County—and one has to be careful, even in the quiet serenity of this place called the Redland. I signed my name and accepted the envelope. The young man smiled and thanked me for taking the letter off his hands as if I had done him a favor. I thought I caught him trying to peer behind the door at the contents of the house, but I didn't let him. It is my home. My sanctuary was affectionately named "*The Hole*" as in, "Gee, Sandy, you sure live in a real hole in the ground." Anybody looking for my home is sure to miss it unless given explicit directions as it is nestled back from the road and situated neatly in the center of five acres conveniently camouflaged by a tangle of Brazilian pepper, slash pines, and bougainvilleas in purple and red with thorns that can catch—and hold— a small animal.

I carried the letter to the kitchen and set it on the table. Part of me wanted to wait to open it. It was fun letting my mind toy with thoughts of winning some contest and being forever stinking rich enough to tell everyone to fuck off, but I knew better. My luck never ran so deep, and there were few people left that I hadn't told to fuck off already. I fixed some coffee and sat down with my prize and carefully opened it foregoing my usual rip and grab the contents of the mail. Already, I was treating it like something special. I decided I needed to get a life if this was how I treated certified letters.

Back in my reality mode, my eyes scanned the page for a name of recognition and found it at the bottom. I shook my head trying to rattle the name from my memory. Clancy. Clancy T. Rodoson. I knew nobody by that last name, but I knew one Clancy Truitt. Her father, Jack, passed himself off as a friend of the family while I was in grade school, and his presence haunted my dreams ever since. He became a focal point of my frustration every year following my escape, and the abuse I suffered at his hands slowly evolved and grew into a ball of unbridled hatred that festered deep within my gut and forced the ungodly taste of bile to the back of my throat.

The letter informed me that Jack was dead and Clancy needed to talk with me about his estate. What could I possibly have to do with the asshole's estate, I wondered? I must have not given it much thought as I threw the paper in the trash.

I grabbed my cup of coffee and headed back to the inner sanctum of my bedroom and fell back to sleep without touching the coffee.

Nearly three hours passed when the phone rang. It was time to get up anyway, I figured, so I took the call instead of letting it go directly to voicemail.

"Hi, Sandy, I am afraid I have some bad news for you." Randy's voice sounded troubled.

"Well, what is it?" I spat. I have had about enough surprises for one day I informed him, and my sleep was already interrupted once for no good reason.

"I think you better get down to Amaretto right away. Pudge is gone— dead."

For a minute, I shook my head and tried to jar the information I had received. Pudge was an old shrimper and a friend of mine for the past five years. I met him while I was writing a story about old-time shrimpers and the lives they led. He was reluctant to let me on his boat to interview him at first, but I brought him a bottle of single malt scotch and threw my backpack over the side of the boat one night, and without taking his hand for assistance, hopped over and proceeded to listen to him spin tales in a drunken stupor the whole night. When the sun came up, we were still talking. Pudge told me the other shrimpers at the dock would think I was a whore that spent the night with him, and he wanted to defend my honor and tell them the truth.

I informed him that members of my own family had called me worse, and I didn't give a shit what he told the others. My honor was nothing he needed to be defending. Hell, if I couldn't defend my own honor, I'd better find another way to make a living. He smiled that gap-toothed smile of his and winked. After publication of the story, I brought a copy to Pudge to get his opinion.

"You made me sound like some kind of folk hero," he said, as a wry smile crossed his weathered lips, "I like that. And thanks for not mentioning all the things I told you not to mention."

Since that time, we became friends—mostly getting drunk and seeing who could spin the longest yarns. I would often go to Amaretto and help him out with whatever needed to be done to the boat. I spent a week there scraping Amaretto's barnacle-encrusted hull last year with Pudge and Randy. It turned into a pretty good chapter of my third book—the dialogue was exquisite and filled with color. Aside from Randy and his wife Susan, Pudge was the only true friend I had in this world, and I couldn't grasp the fact that Pudge's sunbaked creased face would not be at Amaretto the next time I went there.

"Are you there, Sandy? Did you hear me? You're not drunk again, are you?" Randy was getting antsy I could tell.

"You son of a bitch. You don't even let the message sink in, do you? What happened? And no, dearest, I am not drunk. I drink about as much as you do," I lied.

"I'll be over in ten minutes. We have to find out what happened," he said, ignoring my last statement. I think the reason we are good friends is we both have the ability to shrug off each other's bullshit.

"See you then. If there is no answer, I'm in the shower," I replied and hung up. A friendship like ours needs no goodbyes, we determined a long time ago.

Randy and I met in the parking lot of the Wharf Lounge some ten years ago. I staggered out of the bar about one in the morning to find a group of six thugs intent on robbing me, as if I had something to steal. I kicked one of the bastards in the balls and dared the rest to come and get me, and they took me up on it. When in situations like that, I find myself getting extremely brave despite my petite stature. Randy was driving by when he saw the altercation and pulled into the parking lot. He was returning from a spearfishing expedition in the Keys, and he got out of the car armed with a spear gun. I don't think the thugs saw him coming, but Randy managed to shoot one in the leg. Lucky for me, it was the one who had grabbed a fistful of my long hair and was trying to lead me to the tall weeds behind the bar. The spear sticking through his leg caused the others to abandon their mission and the hair-grabber to let go. All of the potential robbers or rapists, save the one lying on the pavement clutching his balls, scattered.

I was rubbing my head when Randy approached and said, "Ever think of getting a haircut?"

I knew then we would become friends. He didn't say, "What's a nice girl like you doing here?" or "Come on, little lady, I'll take you home and make you all better."

I looked up at him and broke out laughing. He did, too. I offered to buy him a drink, but he declined, saying we should call the Florida City cops and report the incident so he could get his spear back. We did, but we found out my life didn't matter to the cops and neither did the spear. Something about the civil rights of the offenders being invaded. I dropped the charges and vowed that if I ever saw any of them again, they wouldn't be able to speak of the meeting as their tongues would be missing. Like I said, I get brave.

Randy and I, and Randy's then-girlfriend, Susan, started diving together, dining together, and confiding and conspiring together. When Randy and Susan decided to get married, they wanted me to be best man, which I couldn't, so we decided on best person.

I think our friendship has survived so well because Randy doesn't ask me why I protested against the Vietnam War in the 1960s, and I don't ask him why he went. Susan just shakes her head at us. She knows there is nothing romantic between us and is secure in knowing there never will be. It is nice to know that in our own little world, different genders can be friends and mean it— despite what other people think.

As I stepped into the shower, my thoughts turned again to Amaretto and Pudge. In that childlike wonder that sometimes surfaces from the cynicism I have cultivated over some forty years, I told myself he would still be there when I got to the dock. And as I stepped from the shower, I began to think about what it was that killed him. The only cause I could muster was too much drink— eventually, it catches up to some people. Mostly the good ones though as the rotten sons of bitches in this world can do just about anything and still live on and on just to make life miserable for the rest of us.

In my bedroom, I found my cleanest dirty jeans and my last clean T-shirt and got dressed. The sunlight found its way through a crack in the blinds, and the beam of light shone across my dresser. In its path lay a golden anchor pendant— the one I always wear. I stopped and stared at it, my gaze transfixed on the hypnotic play of light. It was the anchor Pudge gave me three years ago.

"People of the water are bonded together in ways all others will never know," he said as he gave me the anchor. I picked it up and turned it over in my hand, rubbing it like a magic lamp and wishing for my friend to still be alive. I carefully clasped the chain around my neck and wore the anchor like a talisman.

My Irish setter, Mickey, as in Mickey Dog, gave a hint that Randy had arrived, and I met him in the darkened living room.

"Geez, why don't you fix this place up?"

"What do you suggest? Perhaps gingham curtains and tapestry carpets? I don't have time for domestications, Randy. Besides, if you want to show off your interior decorating expertise, help yourself. I ain't proud."

"Has your son seen this place? He would flip. It looks like a rummage sale in here."

I hesitated a second, wondering what my son had to do with my house in Randy's eyes. I was the one who paid for it, and I was the one who lived here. Why should I worry about who saw my house and what condition it was in when they saw it? Shit. They could always leave or not come in the first place.

"And everything is for sale— name a price," I shot back.

We left the house, still bickering about my lack of housekeeping that culminated with Randy inferring that is the reason I live alone. No one would want to get involved with a cynical writer who can't keep house.

The trip to Amaretto was uneventful and unusually quiet. A couple of times we shared an uneasy glance, but little or no conversation.

We arrived to find Harve, the shrimper in the next slip and a long-time friend of Pudge's, pacing in front of Amaretto.

"Can't believe it," he said, "I heard a shot, and by the time I came over, he was laying over the table."

"What exactly happened?" asked Randy.

"They are saying suicide," a man in a suit answered.

I checked out *The Suit* as he rambled on giving details of Pudge's demise. He appeared to be roughly thirty-five to forty years old with perfectly tailored clothes, shining shoes, and a mop of unruly hair. He thrust a hand in my direction, and without taking a breath, changed the subject from death to a formal introduction.

"Mark Chaney, Mr. Barrington's attorney," he said.

Barrington? I thought it strange to hear Pudge's given name. I thought it even stranger that he had an attorney.

"Sandra Darnell," I said, cautiously taking his hand. He turned to Randy.

"Randy Clark," Randy said as *The Suit* pumped his hand.

"I would appreciate it if you both would come to my office as soon as you get through here. A matter of Mr. Barrington's estate and all. I won't go into great detail here," Chaney said, "because now I believe the police have a few questions they would like to ask you both."

We followed the lawyer under the yellow tape and boarded Amaretto. In the cabin, there were two cops in uniform and two in jeans and T-shirts. The uniformed cops asked us to be seated and proceeded with their formal questioning procedure: "How long did you know the deceased?" "How did you meet?" "Where were you last night?" "Did he have any enemies that you knew of?" "Was he depressed?"

Through the process, my eyes kept straying to the table where Pudge laid his head down and died. It was covered in blood, as were the cabinets and the floor around the chair. I watched as the investigators plucked Pudge's gun from the table and placed it in a plastic bag. I half-listened to what the cops were saying, and my mind began wrestling with the illogical: They are saying that Pudge killed himself. He liked his life. Yet nobody that I know of would want to kill him, and there was no sign of a struggle.

"You can go now. Thanks for your time," one of the cops said as I was beginning to come back to earth.

"You all right?" Randy asked.

I nodded as he said, "Let's go see what the lawyer has to say."

We walked back to the car in silence and said nothing until we pulled onto US1.

"He was murdered, Randy. Somebody killed Pudge," I said.

Randy turned a slow glance my way and asked, "What makes you think that? Nothing was stolen, and there was no sign of a struggle."

"I feel it. And I don't have any answers, but he did not kill himself."

We arrived at Mark Chaney's office and laughed at the irony of its location. The old building housed a Subway at one end, a bait shop and marine electronics shop in the middle, and a shark-shaped wooden sign that stated simply "Mark Chaney, attorney at law."

"Would you go to a lawyer that used a shark as his logo?" Randy asked.

"At least he's got a sense of humor. That's probably why Pudge hired him," I replied.

The lawyer's office was unlike any other I had been in before. There was a very tanned, blonde-haired woman sitting behind a desk in the waiting room. She was wearing a T-shirt that read, "Don't break your family tree— hands off the reefs." Wow, I thought, an environmental legal assistant, what a trip.

"You must be here to talk to my brother about Mr. Barrington, right?" she asked and said at the same time.

"That's right," Randy answered.

"His office is that way," she said and pointed in the only direction we could go without leaving the building.

"Randy, Sandra, good to see you could make it so soon," Chaney said before we even started down the hall.

"Come this way."

He had changed into a pair of shorts and a chambray shirt since the last time we saw him, and he looked much younger than I recalled.

"Sandra …"

"Sandy, please," I corrected.

"Sorry. Sandy, Mr. Barrington—"

"Pudge," I corrected again.

"Sorry—"

"And quit apologizing."

"Sor … right. Okay. Sandy, Pudge left the bulk of his estate to you, including Amaretto and all of its contents. He had a sizable amount of money in the bank— all of which is yours. Here is a copy of his will, if you care to read it." He handed me the papers and I read it through, my eyes rereading several parts that struck my heart particularly hard.

"Excuse me, Mr. Chaney. I need to call my wife," Randy said as he reached for his phone.

"Sure. Go right ahead."

I was amazed that Pudge thought so highly of me. And I was pleased there were humorous interjections in his will. I sighed when I read what Pudge had written about me … "to the lovely dark-haired, dark-eyed woman of the sea, for her years of love and friendship, I, William Henry Barrington III, leave everything I own, both real and personal. She was and is a true friend and the only family I ever needed. Take care of Amaretto and keep those shrimp on the run …"

"Sandy, he wanted to be cremated, so I took the liberty of following his wishes. I hope you don't mind," Chaney said.

"No, that's quite fine," I replied, "I will give his remains a fitting sendoff from Amaretto when the time is right."

"I know you will. He really cared about you, you know that? I don't know what happened to the rest of his family, but I have to start tracking them down. He left his two daughters one hundred dollars each and his ex-wife a letter and five dollars— all symbolic, I am sure. But you are even the beneficiary of his life insurance policy. I will handle all the details for you, so don't worry about anything," the lawyer said.

Randy finished his phone call and asked one last question.

"Why the shark for a business sign? Don't you think that says little about your practice?"

"The shark sign I find quite funny, myself. You see, I used to be a lawyer in Washington, D.C., and I had enough one day and just left. I came here with my sister and started my own practice. It's quiet, and I don't have many clients, but I can fish whenever I want and the weather suits me just fine. I don't regret leaving the big time at all," Chaney said.

For a moment, I set aside my disdain for lawyers and saw a youthful innocence behind the educated face. I could see why Pudge hired him.

As Randy and I made our way back home, a storm swelled in the west and began to pass over the highway. I was thinking about how badly I wanted a drink, but knew better than to say anything to the new and reformed Randy, who rarely, if ever, drank alcoholic beverages anymore.

"Susan is waiting for us at *The Hole*. She went over to feed Mickey and decided the place needed to be cleaned," Randy said.

"I appreciate it, Ran," I mustered.

"Come on, Sandy, tell me what's bugging you."

"He was murdered."

"Don't start that shit again. You can't believe that. Unless there is something you aren't telling me."

"When we get back to *The Hole*, I am going to tell you and Sue something, and then you will believe what I say. Until then, I have nothing else to say."

Randy didn't reply. Maybe it was the tone in my voice that let him know there was no reason to press harder because I was not giving up any more information. I turned my head and stared over Barnes Sound as we drove toward the mainland. And I still wanted that drink.

When we arrived at *The Hole*, Susan was waiting, and I barely recognized my own living quarters. It was clean and neat. The carpet was vacuumed and the dishes were washed. Mickey Dog didn't even get up to greet me; he was stuffed and contented to be sleeping in more suitable surroundings. He opened one eye, saw me, and closed it. So much for Old Faithful.

"You had a couple of phone calls on your landline, Sandy," Susan said. "Two were from someone named Clancy in New Jersey, and one was from your sister, Mary. The other was from your agent who wants to know when the copy will be in— whatever that means."

"Thanks, Sue," I said as I headed to my bedroom.

I closed the door behind me and sat on the edge of my freshly made bed. I thrust my arm deep under the bed and pulled out a bottle of rum and drank a hard gulp. I waited a second and took another. Then I replaced my stash and stared at the wall. I could hear Randy and Susan talking in muffled tones in the living room, but couldn't make out what was said.

I stared at the phone, trying to will it to my ear, but settled for having to reach for it and I dialed my sister's number. She was crying.

"What is it?" I asked. "What's the matter?"

"Daddy's dead. He died about three days ago, but I couldn't get in touch with you."

Funny, I thought, with the exception of Pudge, all these people dying are people I hate—including this one.

"Gee, Sis, that's too bad. I am sorry you lost your father and all, but I have just lost a very dear friend today and am rather upset about that."

"Aren't you a little sad?" she sobbed.

"You want the truth? I am sad. Sad that the sorry, lying, conniving bastard lived as long as he did. I would have been a lot happier had he died, say thirty years ago."

"How can you say that?"

"You know how I can say that. I didn't give a hoot about him then, and I don't give a hoot about him now. Besides, the man that I considered my father died last year, and yes, I was sorry to see him go. But as for your father—he was a waste of human flesh."

"You know, sometimes you are so cold. You need to change your ways or you will be all alone one day. Can't you forgive anyone?"

"Sis, I am alone. And I like it. And it's a little late to go forgiving the bastard that not only screwed up my life, but Mom's and yours— not to mention countless others. So quit with the forgiveness crap, wipe away the tears, and get on with your life."

It was nice the way rum kicks in at the right moment, I thought.

"Well, I just thought you might want to know what happened, that's all," she said.

Poor Mary; she never had a life of her own, I thought. I'll oblige her and let her give me the details of the death of a man I never knew. It would make her feel like she accomplished something.

"Okay, Mar, what happened?"

"He was gardening by the front of his house and a car passed by and hit him. They didn't catch the person who did it."

I had to contain my laughter. I couldn't visualize the old bastard puttering in a garden to begin with. And I damn sure couldn't picture him as road kill either.

"Yeah, well, that's too bad. A real awful way to go. And I truly am sorry for you; I know how much you loved him. I have to get going now, though. Got lots of calls to make. Let me know if there is anything I can do for you. I love you."

I succeeded in cutting her off before I broke out in gut-wrenching guffaws. How about that, I thought, Carlo Anitello, perpetual skirt chaser, who screwed of all my high school girlfriends, and general no-good fuck-up, winds up as road kill in some backward southern state that hated his name, religion, and ethnic background. What a fitting end.

The second call I made was to my agent, Paul Barclay. I told him the manuscript would be in the mail the next day and explained what strange events had happened since the last time we spoke. We agreed that, if all these loose ends somehow fit together, it would make a pretty interesting story. And to that end, we agreed that I would take some time away from deadlines to channel my resources to finding out just what in the hell was going on. No sooner had I hung up the phone then it began that irritating computer chip generated nuisance ring again. I found myself remembering fondly the days when phones actually rang. Now we call it ringing, but it doesn't ring. It irritates, intrudes and— at least for the last twenty-four hours at this number— frays nerves.

"Hello," I answered bitterly.

"Hi, Mom. Just calling to find out how you are," my son said.

"I'm doing fine, Kid. What's up with you?" I braced for what was coming. One thing that has never changed over the years is that most kids never call home for no reason. He wanted something, and it was my proper role as a parent to play the game.

"Shannon and I have something we want to tell you."

"Well, what is it?"

"We want to come over and tell you, if that's okay."

"Sure. And Shane, don't you come over here asking for money, or food, or laundry, or anything else," I said, figuring I eliminated most of what he was going to come over and "tell" me as in "I'm telling you, I sure do miss your cooking, cleaning, et cetera."

"Don't worry, Mom, we wouldn't do that. See you in a bit."

As I hung up the phone, I thought back to ten months ago. I had such dreams for Shane, and he was getting off to a real bad start. One thing I remember from when I was seventeen, almost eighteen, was that I had to take care of Shane. And here, at the very same age was a growing man that had met some giggly goofball who wore her permed hair in a ponytail on the side like a little girl. The whole look was made worse by using some foam hair tie in sickening colors that looked like a string of barf trying to choke a flood of multi-colored brown, blonde, and red tangles from spilling onto her shoulder. I attributed her lack of brains to her hair being pulled to the side too tightly, and she didn't even get what I was talking about. She just stared at me with that vacuous look and said, "I used to wear it looser, but it kept falling down." I wondered what he saw in her. I also wondered if her parents admitted that this was indeed their offspring. He told me he was going out one night and when he came home he told me how much he loved this girl he was seeing. I had no idea it was the ponytail twit, but I was not one to reckon with young love. He informed me that he would be a lot happier living with his older friends and the twit in a shared apartment. Maybe it was my fault he had been living with her for the last ten months. I let him go and I was alone again.

Solitude. I found it refreshing, in a way. The first night, I ran the spectrum of emotions— loneliness, self-pity, anger and hurt. But, I spent the night writing and the following day sleeping, and when I awoke, I was refreshed and no longer frazzled. I had nobody to answer to but me, and I could do what I wanted, when I wanted. I was alone, finally, and happy. I must admit, I did think an awful lot about Lee that night. However, he had been dead going on ten years, and when I am alone, that wanting still digs deep. I thought about how happy we were during our brief years together. He even endured living with the one thing I could not give— the pure unbridled emotionalism that I never was able to muster. I was happy, but it was a muted, controlled happy, and it had to be enough for him. And then he died. Did it break my heart? Yes. Did I let it show? No. I never let emotions show. If I find myself slipping into a teary reverie, I either catch myself and stop it, or I go somewhere alone and cry it out. But I am not about to let those emotional outbursts show to anybody, and I have been called a cold bitch, or the ice lady, too many times to mind anymore. Funny thing, names. I have rolled over in my mind time and time again why it is that a strong, unemotional male is "in control of the situation" or "strong," but a woman of the same virtues is "bitch" or "frigid." Ah, some things I cannot change, I told myself.

I left my bedroom and appeared in the living room as Susan was bringing out snacks.

"Why have you come over here, cleaned up, and cooked for me?" I asked.

"It needed to be done, Sandy. Randy and I were talking. We don't think you should be alone tonight, with Pudge's death and all. I'll stay with you tonight, if you want. I don't have to work tomorrow, and Randy has to go in early."

I sincerely appreciated the concern. And I knew if Susan stayed with me, we could talk about "girl things" and get shit-faced drunk. Nothing better I would like to do at this time anyway.

"Sure. Whatever. But you really don't have to. I'll be quite all right, I am sure."

"It is settled then. I am staying," Susan insisted.

I was happy that I wouldn't have to be alone.

Shane pulled into the drive as I was about to place a second fried mushroom in my mouth. His dipshit girlfriend bounded out of the car after him like a loyal puppy with an off-centered tail.

They came into the house as if he still lived here.

"Hi, Mom, how are you?" my truly handsome son asked. And, for a moment, I was pitched back in time to the day he was just a boy. My God, how time does play hide-and-seek with us. It creeps up and grabs us whether we are ready or not.

"Have a seat, Shane. Want some mushrooms?" I was trying to ignore Shannon. Her face was pulled back tighter than I ever remembered.

"How are things going at the animal farm?" I couldn't resist asking the question. After all, the nearest I could figure, he was living with at least five others in a two-bedroom apartment.

"Oh, Mom. Things are going just fine. We all do our part. Of course, nobody can cook like you. I do miss that. And I am waiting for that invitation to dinner."

"We hope that we can spend more time with you real soon," piped Shannon.

That sealed it. They were never coming to dinner.

"What is it that is so important, Shane?" I had a shitty day and was anxious to get rid of them yet still maintain politeness.

"Well," he said, holding Shannon's hand and looking at her glowingly. "We are going to have a baby. We figured we'd get married in the next couple of months."

If I were an emotional person, I would have lost my mushroom. But, I am not, and I kept my dinner.

"Yes. We are going to have a baby," Tight-head squeaked, "And you are going to be a grandmother. This way, you won't have to be alone anymore during the day. You can be your grandchild's own daycare center. Isn't that wonderful?"

Boy that mushroom was getting closer to my lips from the inside.

"I really don't think so, Shannon. I raised my kid. He's out of here now. This is yours, and you will raise it. The last thing I want is another child. If I wanted another, I would have had one. But, I didn't want one, and I didn't have one. I don't want yours, and I ain't no daycare center or babysitter. Looks like you will have to do as I did— fork over money to a *real* center and a *real* sitter."

"But, we both have to work," she sniveled.

"So did I, Child. And I was alone when he was a baby. I managed. If you need help, ask your own parents," I said, maintaining my cool.

"Oh, no," she said, "they will never understand. They think I am too young. I don't know if we will tell them right away.

Besides, they both are professionals and have all this responsibility and stuff. They aren't like you. You get to work from home."

"I have to leave home almost every month. I do a lot of research and traveling."

"She's right, Shan," Shane interrupted. "My mother isn't home that much. And she is a professional, too. We will find a way to work it out, don't worry."

Then an amazing thing happened. Shannon began whining. Whining like my mother's cousin always whined. Actually, it was a trait she passed to her children, too—a whole family of wop whiners. I thought this grating-on-my-nerves whining was limited to Italians, and I had seen the last of the whiners, but no, the whiner from hell was sitting right here in my house—at my table.

"But, you always told me she was nice. She has never said one nice thing to me. Doooo something, pleeease."

I gave Shane my best mean and aggravated look to warn him I was about to fire my mouth. He braced himself.

"Look, quit whining, because I have no tolerance for that. It may work with Mr. and Mrs. Upper-Middle-Class-Two BMW's-And-The-World-Owes-Us-Something-Yuppie who gave birth to the spoiled little WASP brat, but it don't cut it here. Look at you and ask yourself if you are really ready for this baby you are having. You don't even have the flutters in your belly, and you are trying to pawn the kid off on an adult. You ain't playing house here. You are going to be responsible for a human life who will be totally dependent on you. You think you can just intrude in my life and tell me I will be your child's guardian angel? That shows how much maturity you have. Now, you will see what the real consequences of romantic, spontaneous, teenage fuck-fests are all about. Have fun. Keep working and save your money. Welcome to the real world and enjoy it. And one more thing, if you keep pulling your hair back like that, your face will stay that way— all stretched to one side. Do you know how stupid you look? I hope your kid favors my son. That's all I have to say except, Shane, next time you come to visit— come alone— or don't come at all."

I got up from the table and went back to my rum bottle asking myself what I did to deserve this.

In between the argument and the rum, I became tired. Tired of hearing of all the strange circumstances surrounding Pudge's demise that I tried to piece together. Tired of my son and his dipshit significant other. And, most unbelievably, tired of hearing that my enemies were all dropping like flies. I fell asleep.

When I woke, the house was quiet and not quite dark. I rubbed my eyes and staggered to the living room, drawn like a moth to the soft evening light coming from the patio. Susan was sitting in the near dark, smoking a cigarette and looking out to some far away galaxy. She looked so serene in her meditation. Her straight blonde hair fell limply around her shoulders, and her delicate features glowed under the simple light. I could see why Randy fell in love with her. Susan was a constant in our triad. Never angry or depressed, she was simply Susan— all the time.

Randy and I had our mood swings. Intense and fierce sparring on occasion and deep fits of depressed silence. We were so much alike, Susan thought we were long lost siblings— and we fought as such many times. She never took sides and never interfered. Susan just got up and walked away shaking her head at our spats. If only I could find a mate with the same qualities, I would be totally contented, but I knew that would never happen. Susan was unique. I would still be me, and much like Randy, as always, I would find something to bitch about. He did. He complained about Susan constantly. "What the hell are you looking for?" I once asked him.

"Something else. That's all," he replied, sounding so much like me it was frightening.

"You're awake," Susan said as I opened the patio door.

"Barely," I replied.

"I got rid of the kids. Boy, am I glad I don't have any. Where did your son find the bimbo anyway?"

"I have no idea and I am afraid to ask."

"What a shame. They think it will be so easy. They have no idea what is in store for them," Susan said in a sympathetic way.

"Well, it's never too early to grow up. I wish them well."

There was a fresh pot of coffee on the table and a cup. Susan was the perfect housemate. I decided that the next time Randy uttered a word of discontent about her, I would hurt him.

We sat there in silence for a short time— Susan looking into space and me wishing I was on the ocean somewhere far away from land and all people. It was a clear November night, still and humid. I was thankful for Indian summers. The night air wrapped around us like a warm, moist blanket. There was a trace of a breeze coming from the southeast, but not a cooling breeze. It was a salty breeze bringing droplets of seawater to *The Hole* and surrounding me in that all too familiar scent of the ocean. My thoughts came back to land only for a second as Susan remarked on how long the summer had been. Here it was November, and we were still wallowing in September weather. It didn't bother me, I told her. And it wouldn't bother me if it stayed this way forever. It never ceased to amaze me how people who lived here could bitch about the weather constantly: too hot, too humid, no seasons. Yet when asked, each of them revealed why they came here in the first place: the weather. Goes to show people will bitch about anything, especially things they can't change.

"Randy said you had a hunch about Pudge and were going to tell us what it was when you got home," Susan said breaking my train of weather thought.

"Right. I got sidetracked when my kid and the dipshit came over."

I thought about what I was going to say. I wanted to say it right the first time knowing I would have to repeat it for Randy at a later time. I hate having to tell the same story over and over. I find it boring. Like seeing the same bad movie time after time and finding, much to your horror, that you are remembering the dialogue. And the words follow you, popping into your head at the most inopportune times.

"Well, this is why I believe he was murdered," I began, "We all know Pudge was basically a contented person; he had Amaretto, loved to spend time on the sea, had no close family to harass him. and, come to find out, a great deal of money. He also had us. Good friends that cared about him and were not above going out to give him a hand when he had no mates. He had no reason to kill himself. I remember him telling me one night that he spent a great deal of time molding his life into something he wanted. And this was what he wanted. There were no haunts left. No spooks to catch him in the middle of the night. If I get to Amaretto tomorrow, I can prove he was murdered." I added the last sentence after peering into Susan's narrowing eyes. She doubted what I was saying, I could tell. Call it a hunch. She fumbled in her pockets for a joint. By the growing redness around her eyes, I could tell it wasn't her first.

"Don't tell Randy," she said as she lit it and sucked hard. She offered it to me, but I declined as I always do. I'm more of an alcohol-high-loving person.

"Sandy," she said as she exhaled, "none of us want to believe Pudge killed himself. I know you are upset about him. So am I. So is Randy. But there is no reason not to believe he did away with himself. We all have the ability. What is there on Amaretto that can prove your theory?"

I hesitated to tell her about "the box." It was Pudge's secret. And I couldn't bring myself to reveal his secret even if he was dead. Before I opened my mouth again, I said a silent prayer to the spirit of Pudge asking forgiveness for letting this pass my lips.

"There is a secret hold on Amaretto. In the hold, there is a small Oriental rosewood box inlaid with jade and sealed with a brass lock. In that box is a stash of emeralds and gold coins."

Susan's red-rimmed eyes widened.

"Where did Pudge get that stuff?"

"We were out setting traps one lobster season about three years ago. Me and Pudge and Steve the Slime. The seas were rough, about eight to ten that day, when one of the swells caught Amaretto and sideswiped her, washing over the decks and tossing several traps overboard. I offered to dive for the traps, but Pudge insisted I not go down alone and ordered Steve to go with me. Steve refused and a fistfight broke out."

I paused there for a minute recalling the fight. I remember it well. I was trying in vain to get my gear together in the tossing boat when we hit another swell, and I wound up taking an upper cut to the jaw that was meant for Pudge. I toppled back and fell, cutting the shit out of my head. I didn't know it at the time, but when I did go over, the salt stung so bad, I lost my breath.

"While the fighting progressed," I continued, "I went to the bow, said a prayer that I could make the drop without losing my gear, and strode over losing only one fin, but recovering it quickly. I was over weighted so I could sink quickly and found a trap line and followed it down. I was getting whipped back and forth the whole way down, but I managed to hug the bottom long enough to retrieve most of the other traps. I tied them together and was getting ready to pull them back up the line when something caught my eye. I went over and couldn't believe my eyes. There, in plain sight, lay a cache of emeralds and gold coins! I plucked the largest emerald and one coin and tucked it in my BC pocket before bringing the traps up. When I approached the surface, I saw a light Pudge dropped over to let me know he was expecting me, so I went to the stern and he threw me a line.

Steve was lying on the deck, his nose bleeding. "I knocked him out," Pudge told me. "Good," I said.

"After we got the traps on board, Pudge wanted to leave. The seas were getting worse. I told him to wait and showed him what I found. His eyes widened and he grinned that shit-eating grin. But, Pudge being the protective person he was, wouldn't let me back down alone, so we waited for Steve to come around, and we both went down for the rest."

"I can't believe this," Susan said. "Of all the times not to have Randy around! Steve the Slime had to be there. I never did trust that bastard. So what happened?"

"I kept watching Steve. He was loading up his pockets as he was placing pieces into the bag. I guess he figured he'd take his cut before Pudge and I killed his ass for the fight and all— which, I might add, did cross my mind a time or two already. I was as fed up with his bullshit as was Pudge, and I would have welcomed the sight of Steve gasping for air as the swells washed over him."

I told Susan how when we got to the surface, we had about three dozen emeralds and forty gold coins bearing a royal Spanish inscription. A lost part of the 1715 fleet that met its demise during a hurricane, no doubt. The seas, stirred by the squall we were in, revealed a long-hidden secret. We decided we would tell nobody about the cache. Later, when we returned to the slip and Steve was on his way, I told Pudge about his loaded BC. Pudge figured as much, but brushed it off as Steve just being Steve. Then he asked me how much of the treasure I wanted. I told him I didn't care for any of it; I'd probably lose it anyway. That was when he showed me the hiding place. He pulled the box from the niche and placed all the emeralds and coins in an old white sock and locked them in the box. He told me if I ever needed them, that's where they would be. And we vowed never to tell anyone where they were.

"So, let me get this straight; you think Steve came back, found Pudge, shot him, and took the loot?" Susan asked.

I nodded.

"But why would Pudge tell him where it was hidden? You know as well as I that he could be extremely tight-lipped." She looked at me as she said those words, giving me a glare that burned right through me. She crushed out the joint and only after it was extinguished to her satisfaction did she remove the stare from me.

It heaved up a memory of infidelity on the part of Randy. Susan came into the Pilot House in Key Largo one night looking for Randy, but finding only me and Pudge. She asked where he was, and we both shrugged. At that precise moment, Randy ventured in with Luellen on his arm. It was a scene I never want to repeat. Not only did Randy catch hell from Susan, but Pudge and I got in our licks as well for putting us in the middle. When Pudge asked Randy what he saw in Luellen in the first place, Randy looked at him and muttered one word: "tits" and shrugged. I think it was the only time I saw a side of Randy I hated. Like no other woman had tits. Like Susan's tits were somewhat less than he was worth? I got him back for that remark some time later. We were working Amaretto again, and he said something about my lack of love life. I just looked at him as he went on about how I needed a man to satisfy my sexual hunger— a man who knew what he was doing. I caught Pudge glancing over smiling and shaking his head at Randy's remarks. I chose to raise one eyebrow in amusement at Randy's expertise in knowing what I wanted and needed.

Finally, I asked Randy what made him think he knew all about women's desires anyway. He said, "Men just know what women want and what they need and how to deliver. It's in their blood or something."

This really made me laugh. And I was pleased that Pudge joined in.

"I really hate to bust your little fantasy here, Ran. But there ain't nothing you or any other man can do for me that I can't do better myself," I said, "and, I might add, with a whole lot less aggravation attached. You see, I can deal with waking up next to me in the morning, but I don't think I could stand waking up to some egotistical bullshit artist who thinks he knows what he is doing, when he doesn't, and then turns around one day and says, 'Gee, Luellen has better tits; I'll go get some of those.'"

Pudge about pissed on the deck when I said that, and Randy's face turned so red we thought it would blister.

So, I knew what Sue was thinking when she gave me that evil stare. Because just like she could say anything to me about Randy and/or her innermost feelings, so too, could Randy. I made a vow that never the two shall hear it from my lips. And that was the secret of our friendship.

"Well, the Slime had the motive," Sue continued, "and, I haven't seen him in a long, long time which could mean he left and then decided to come back for the stash thinking we all forgot about him. But, until I see the empty hold, I won't believe it."

"But, what do *you* believe, Sue?" I asked. At this point, I was willing to hear any and everything.

"I believe Pudge just got tired. That's all. He decided to end it while he still had that fire about him. He wouldn't have wanted to wither away or anything. I think he did it."

The nagging phone interrupted our conversation, again. Jeez, the damned thing never stopped. Sue jumped up and got it thinking it was Randy, but it wasn't. I heard her talking and went in.

"Here she is. And you take care of yourself and have a nice time," Sue said into the receiver. "It's your mother calling from France," she said as she handed me the phone.

"Mom! How are you? Are you having a good time?" I truly was excited to hear her voice again. I really missed not having her around to talk to when I was between projects.

"I'm fine; what is new there?" she asked in a rested voice. I told her about the strange happenings. She chuckled at the road kill in Georgia and scolded me for talking the way I did to my sister. I told her about Jack Truitt and she seemed to take it in stride. Old friends die, she said unemotionally, and there is nothing we can do about it.

I didn't bother to tell her how much I despised that bastard. In time, I figured. She asked about her house, and I assured her it was still standing and in good shape for her return. She told me she wasn't planning to come home for a while and apologized for the imposition of placing me in charge of her bills. It was really the least I could do for her, and I was happy she decided to take the six-month trip. She didn't know Pudge, so I didn't tell her about his death, but I did tell her about Shane and Shannon. I was prepared for a lecture of "how could you let this happen," but it never came.

"Well," she said, "he's old enough to bump his nose."

A kid and a spoiled brat girlfriend is a hell of a nose bump, I thought, but I let it go. There was nothing her beloved grandson could do wrong. We exchanged a few other pleasantries before cutting the conversation short. I was proud of her. She is one hell of a woman, I thought. There is nothing that can stop her. She is truly a mistress of immense strength.

As soon as I hung up the phone, it rang again. This time it was Randy. I retold the story of the secret hold before giving the phone to Susan. They spoke for about ten minutes. This time, as soon as Sue hung up the phone, it rang again, and she figured it was Randy calling to tell her something he forgot. But, my bad luck was higher than spring tide during a full moon. It was Clancy, and there was no getting out of talking to her this time.

"You are a hard person to track down," she said in that giddy voice that hadn't changed in twenty years.

"It's intentional," I snipped.

If I had wanted to be found by the demons of a past life in New Jersey, I would not have changed my name and had an unpublished telephone number. The people I knew in Florida were just fine, even the shitheads, but the people that I knew from way back then, the small town losers, I had little or no tolerance for. They hated me when I was living there and gave my mother immense grief for being the only single mother in town whose husband didn't die. They thought that the only true measure of success in life was marrying a small town pea-brain to rule the roost while women raised a brood of small town conformists to grow up and continue the cycle. There was no room for an artist like my mother or a writer like me. I thought I would suffocate in the shadow of New York and thought for sure I would die at the hands of Jack Truitt's abuse or wind up killing the bastard eventually. So

I figured the only thing to do was leave, which I did. I just disappeared without a reason when I was still too young to be aware of the danger and too old to remain under the thumb of a perverted "family friend."

Eventually, I found my way to Miami in search of warmth and anonymity. I found both. I changed my name, became *pane bianco*, and bought *The Hole* with the royalties from my first book. Along the way, I learned to play a mighty good game of poker and made some good friends and a few enemies. But I survived. I lived in Los Angeles and New Orleans for a while before I wound up a pregnant teen in Florida. And before that, I did the rounds of the small southern towns that were even worse than Berkeley, which I thought was impossible. Each of the places I lived never felt like home. *The Hole* was and always would be my home. It was the only place that didn't feel like giant hands gripping my throat choking the very life out of me. I could breathe here, and when I needed to get away, there was always a quick trip to the Caribbean or simply an outing with Pudge and Randy.

We all— Randy, Susan, Pudge, and I— spoke one night of how we all came here by accident. We decided that nobody except very old people and Canadians came to South Florida on purpose. Everyone wound up here by a tangle of circumstances. Pudge came here to buy a shrimper and take it back to Mobile, but never went back after buying Amaretto. Randy came here from Malibu to go diving and never returned after seeing his first reef. Susan came here from Mississippi with an old boyfriend who abandoned her for a kilo of cocaine. And I came to visit mom one day and was smitten by the lure of the ocean and the wetness of the summer night air.

"Are you there?" Clancy asked.

"Not really. Look, what is it do you want and why can't you take a major hint?" I really decided I had had enough of her.

"Well, my father left you some stuff. and I thought I should get it to you."

"Take it and do one of two things with it: shove it or toss it in the Passaic. I really have no time for this, Clancy," I said, although I could tell she was not going to give up.

"I know it's not much, but some of the things may mean something to you. There are things that belonged to your family and all."

"Such as?" I asked.

"A bunch of crystal and some pieces of silver," she replied.

Oh, joy, I thought, even more reason to hate him; he was a thief. I was sure my blood pressure was about to blow the top of my head off when I caught Clancy's words about the cops not finding any clues yet in Jack's murder, and it hit me like an anvil: until then, I assumed Jack died a natural death— sons of bitches always do with the exception of my biological father.

"Did you say murder, Clancy? What happened, if you don't mind telling me," I purred coyly.

She seemed relieved that I didn't toss another insult her way and politely obliged.

"He was driving home from my house when someone ran him off the road through the Indian Reservation," she began. "Witnesses said the car that sideswiped him had out of state plates, but couldn't say from where. It was as if they knew who they were after. They tailed him for quite a while and made sure he would go down the side of a mountain. The cops say it was definitely murder, but there seems to be no motive."

My hands started to sweat.

Two random traffic homicides in less than a week killing two people that I hated topped by the murder of someone that I loved. Something was telling me these incidents were all tied together, but there was no common denominator.

"Clancy, wrap everything up in a box and mail it to me," I said, trying to remain calm and hoping the contents of the package would yield a clue.

"All right, I'll do that," she said.

"And Clancy …"

"Yes."

"After you do that. Forget you ever knew me. Because I still don't like you," I said and hung up. Okay, so I still was a rude, crude, and ornery person. I could see no reason to change.

Susan was still next to me when I hung up. I looked at her, she looked at me, and we both knew we shared a common thought.

"Too fucking weird for me," she said, high from the weed. "Too fucking

weird."

"Sue, take time off from work. You and me and Randy are going to get to the bottom of this shit, if it kills me," I said.

She smiled and called Randy.

Chapter 2

The Dream

It was nearing three when I decided that I should get some sleep. An avowed insomniac, I only slept when my body could no longer stand being awake. Sometimes, it would take three or four days before I finally slept for five hours straight. This night, I lay awake for a while, my mind racing to the corners of the universe, before finally dozing. I was aware of my surroundings, not fully asleep when "*The Dream*" started.

There are few things in life that truly scare me, and *The Dream* is one of them. It's probably because in its motion picture graphic reality, the major star—a snake—is another thing that scares me. Oh, it isn't an ordinary snake. It is a very thick snake with evil eyes. It seems to be about twenty-feet long, bright purple in color, and, unlike most snakes, has no scales. It feels soft, almost velvet-like, and it comes from an abyss, silently sneaking up on me as I float naked in the air. There is no sky, no water, and no earth around me. The snake just appears around my left ankle. At first, the feeling is calming and not the least bit threatening, like a velvet cloth running around my lower leg. Then I look down and see what it is and panic. The head of the snake appears and those green eyes meet mine. They are wild and hungry like a panther ready to pounce. I try to pull my leg free, but the serpent's grip tightens and pulls me into the abyss. I know I don't want to go where it leads, but there is nothing to hold on to. I claw the air trying to free myself. I open my mouth and try to scream, but nothing comes out.

I awoke in a pool of cold sweat.

I was not aware that I had slept until the sun was just breaking over the horizon. I sat up and looked around my room. Mickey Dog was snoring on the foot of the bed and seemed undisturbed by my getting up. I went to the kitchen, fixed the coffee, and went outside to watch morning unfold over *The Hole*. In the morning mist, I forgot about *The Dream* and took a pen and pad and jotted down my planned course of action.

The first thing I needed to do was get to Amaretto. I decided to go alone and wait there for Randy to get off work. Why is it, I asked myself, that my plans are always so grand, so perfect when I write them down? Nothing could possibly go wrong, and if it did, there was an alternative plan to pick up the slack. Then reality kicks in, and I realize I can't do a damned thing until all the other gears synchronize and get the show moving. I did my laundry instead.

By the time Susan awoke, I had finished my chores and even washed Mickey. I told her I was going to head down to Amaretto and for her and Randy to meet me there when he got off work. I needed to be alone for a while anyway, as if I didn't have enough solitude under normal circumstances at *The Hole*. Sometimes, I would be alone for a week, not going out and not having anyone come over. I liked it that way. As I headed south on US1, I thought more of my aloneness. I wondered mostly about people who always needed people around them to feel whole. Poor bastards, I thought, they probably couldn't stand themselves and that is why they had to have people near them— to keep from thinking about how miserable they were and how they hated their lives. Then I thought about Shane. I was glad he was happy, if he was happy. God knows I was less than a great mother to him. I remember him coming home from school crying because his classmate called him a bastard. Hell, I didn't know who his father was, and I couldn't pretend. So I made up a mythical man and told Shane his father died in an accident. I really can't remember him ever bringing the subject up to me again, but I did overhear him telling the story to another schoolmate once. I hoped he would be a better parent than I was. As for the bimbo, I decided she was not that bad for Shane, but I still would rather not see her and her weird hair again.

The docks were quiet when I arrived at Amaretto. There were only three commercial trawlers behind Key Largo Fisheries now. Pudge had moved Amaretto up from Key West a year ago when the dockage at the Bight went high enough to cut into his profits. Someone had hung a wreath of white roses on Amaretto's rust-stained stern. I figured it was Harve and the rest of the guys and was pleased to find out I was right. Harve waved as I approached. He shook his head, his mop-like hair swinging. "Won't be the same here without ol' Pudge. We figgered it was the least we could do, hangin' that wreath there. Amaretto's yours now. Hope you love her as much as Pudge did and remember we are all here for you— to care for Amaretto and look after her."

He put his arm around my shoulder and squeezed. We had all lost someone dear. In a short time, Don and Mike came over, and we stood there looking at Amaretto like we were waiting for Pudge to appear on her deck. Slowly, they left, one by one, with Harve being the last to leave me alone. Amaretto's bilges kicked in spewing yellow-orange water from her insides. I smiled. I remember Pudge telling me why he named her Amaretto in the first place.

"See that, she looks like she's peeing Amaretto into the water. Aye. Amaretto."

Aye. Amaretto. I mouthed the words to myself as I boarded her. So empty, these decks now that I was alone here. I went into the cabin and was surprised to find that Harve and company had cleaned most of the blood from the table. They also straightened her up. Funny, I thought, these past two days everybody has been cleaning for me. I spent time rummaging around, avoiding the secret hold. I groped for Pudge's sextant and fiddled with the cold brass for a while. I looked through some old charts in the chart room and found his journals. He was quite a writer, filling his journals with minute details of his adventures. I found the journal with the notes of our first meeting in it. "… She blew onto the deck like she owned the place and prodded me with questions. But she had some fine scotch with her and she could drink as well as anyone. She suffered in her life, I could tell it in her eyes. I wonder if my eyes revealed anything to her? What did she want with an old fisherman anyway, and who did she think she was? She stole my heart. And she's honest, I can tell."

Then I found another entry that surprised me:

"Took some comfort with Josephine this Saturday. What a strange woman, but kind. The boy is strong and has my eyes. I wonder if she ever told him the truth."

I wrinkled my brow. I knew Pudge had two daughters and was divorced a long time, but I never recalled him saying anything about a son or a Josephine. I checked that date of the journal, and it wasn't more than a year old. What other secrets did he have?

I found my way to Pudge's bunk and placed his old cap on my head. I had dragged some of the journals with me and put my feet up to get comfortable. I reached under the bunk, found a half-pint of rum, and drank some. It was almost like he expected me to reach under there and find it. Before long, I found my eyes getting heavy from the rum and reading, and I fell asleep propped up on Pudge's bunk with the smell of sea and fish in my nose and the taste of rum in my mouth. And I dreamed *The Dream* again.

Randy woke me as the snake was pulling me down and saw fear on my face.

"What happened? Nightmare?" Randy asked as if he didn't know by the terror in my eyes.

I rubbed my eyes and removed the cap. "Yeah, same old one. Been having it for a long time."

"The snake?"

"The snake."

"You know," he said in that authoritative way he had, "You might should go to a shrink or something to find out what that dream is all about. Susan said it could have something to do with your childhood."

"Sue took too many psychology courses in college. Besides, I went to a shrink once. Never told her about the snake, but just the same, she decided I have this problem with my childhood. Like I didn't fucking know that before. Told me I was mad about my father abandoning the family. I told her I was mad about him fucking all my high school friends. She told me I was mad at Jack for raping me when I was nine, and I told her I was mad at Jack for lying to my whole family about what a caring friend he was. In short, she said I had a lot of problems. I told her there was nothing wrong with me—at least nothing that a .38 couldn't handle.

"Then she assumed I was suicidal. I told her I wouldn't shoot me, you fool, I'd shoot the other bastards."

"So you stopped going?"

"Look, I don't need an analyst to tell me my life is fucked up. I already know that. What I do need is a good night's sleep and maybe a fine steak dinner."

Randy smiled and slowly shook his head.

"You are a real prize, you know that?"

"Yeah, a winner," I agreed. "And now that all the people I hate are dead, my life is truly peachy."

I pulled myself up from the bunk and stashed the rum bottle back where it belonged. I knew I would need it again soon as long as weird things kept happening.

Randy followed me out to the deck and squinted. "So?" he asked, "Is the box there?"

"I didn't look. I wanted to wait for you to get here."

"Afraid of creepy things that might go bump in the night?" he asked sarcastically as he wiggled his fingers in front of my eyes.

"You, of all people, should know that I am not afraid of creepy bullshit. I choose to base everything on logic. And if there is no logic to prove it, then it remains trickery, pure and simple. Bullshit and nothing more."

"You hard ass. Even I fall for mystique now and then."

"*That*, my friend, is your problem."

I moved toward the table where Pudge's head lay as he died and slid it over about a foot. The floor under the table was clean and polished like the rest of the floor used to be in Amaretto's past life. I slid a sharp knife between the third and fourth clean planks and lifted. The hinges creaked as if they hadn't been opened in a long time. There, sitting in the hold, was the space where the rosewood box had been. But it wasn't there. I looked up at Randy.

"The Slime did it," he said, referring to the name we gave Steve because of his lack of hygiene.

I remained staring into the gaping hole that held Pudge's and my secret. Slowly, I raised my head and faced Randy.

"I don't know, Ran. Steve didn't know the stash was here. Only me and Pudge knew. And I damned sure didn't kill him. Although, if anybody finds out about the treasure, I am sure I would have the perfect motive. Gee, that makes me feel like shit."

"Nah," Randy said, "Everybody knows that all you had to do was ask Pudge for anything, and he would give it to you. He really loved you. Lord knows, I don't know why— the bitch you are."

And he smiled. Good thing, too. I was in no mood for jokes.

"You know, Steve could have come back," he continued, "and threatened Pudge into telling him where the stash was. A gun can be pretty persuasive as you well know."

Randy was talking about one of our all-night poker games that we usually held in the back of noted grills and bars in the Keys. We would round up gamblers and play for high stakes. One night, we wound up playing with a bunch of out-of-towners. We figured they would be easy targets for a month's worth of bucks. And they were—at first. Then things started to happen. When we called it a night and stood up to leave, the ringleader pulled a .44 and held it in my face. He demanded I continue playing, which I did. And I made sure I lost every dollar I had won and then some. When we left, Randy asked me how I managed to stay so calm as he had figured we were as good as dead. At that moment, I began to tremble. I only shake in hindsight, I said. It's too risky to panic during the altercation. And it is incredible what staring down the barrel of a loaded gun does for your psyche; it clears all the cobwebs.

"I doubt Steve had the balls for that. Don't forget all the other guys that were around that night. None of the boats were out. But, it wouldn't hurt to track him down," I said. "By the way, where is Sue?"

"She'll be here later. She went to get provisions. Someone's got to think of food, you know."

We replaced the hatch and the table in their original positions and rummaged through Amaretto looking for something, anything, that would help us. We were digging through Pudge's pockets when Randy said something that burned into me.

"You know, maybe these things are all tied together."

"What things?" I asked.

"Well, seems to me that you have had some strange phone calls about people dying. Maybe they are tied to this," he shrugged his shoulders and gave me that creased-eye look.

"Suppose you tell me how the death of two people I hate, both in different states, ties in with the death of a friend here? I ain't no gumshoe, but I don't believe that they could possibly be related."

"Always the fucking skeptic. Listen, maybe you are in danger here. Maybe you pissed someone off. We both know you have that ability. Maybe these are all warnings for you. Hell, I don't know, but I just got a bad feeling. And those weird snake dreams you always have. Shit, I'm scared for you."

Randy reached out for me, and I went to him. It was weird, but I never thought of it the way he did. And if the thought did enter my mind, I swept it out with logic before it planted the seed of doubt in my mind. I fell against Randy's chest and wrapped my arms around him. His chest heaved under my cheek, and I felt warm and secure in his embrace.

"You know, it's really all right to be afraid. And sad. It's okay to cry, and I won't tell anyone."

I closed my eyes and tried to squeeze out some tears, but they wouldn't fall. I tried to remember the last time I cried and couldn't. I wished with all my might that I could just explode in unbridled tears, but they didn't come. I settled for squeezing my arms around Randy's lanky body.

"Yo! Am I interrupting anything here?" Sue asked. With her catlike walk, she came on board unnoticed.

"Yeah," Randy answered. "I was trying to make time with Sandy. Wanna watch?"

"That might be amusing," she answered, unthreatened.

Sue started unpacking a bag of food and began making sandwiches.

"So? What did my two investigators find? Any answers?"

"More questions, Sue," Randy answered. "The loot is missing."

Susan's eyes looked at Randy, then at me.

"Steve the Slime did it," she said in a very matter-of-fact tone.

"After lunch, we're all going to Key West and try to find him," Randy said as if we had discussed this. "Just to find out what he's been up to." He smiled and continued, "You know, a bath maybe. Maybe murder. If he's living the high life, then we'll know something is up anyway."

Sue took two bites from her sandwich and looked at me not eating.

"You got something against ham?" she asked.

"No, just not hungry. Tired, but not hungry," I answered.

"She had the snake dream again," Randy told Sue. "When I got here, she was dreaming about the snake."

I was bracing for Susan to tell me what Randy already did about the shrink and was taken aback by what fell out of her mouth.

"Since we're going to Key West, we might should stop in and visit with *The Moon Lady*. Maybe she has an answer to *The Dream*. And maybe she's seen Steve."

"Oh no. I am not spilling my guts to *The Moon Lady*. She's a nutcase, Susan. You can't possibly believe in that charlatan! Give me a break," I said in my strongest protest.

The Moon Lady was a strange old bird who held court at the No Name Pub Bar on No Name Key. And like the Key she frequented, we assumed she had no name. We called her The Moon Lady.

She was a big woman in her sixties or seventies with small hints of dyed hair peeking out from a tight multi-colored turban. She always wore a muumuu and adorned herself with baubles and beads so when she walked, she clanked and jingled. She was fond of vodka and wine, and I never saw her out of the bar. She had a face as round as the full moon and large gold earrings hung almost to her shoulders. She was truly a frightening character. She hauled tarot cards around in her deep cleavage and was forever telling people's fortunes for a price. My eyes widened at the prospect of sitting across a barroom table from *The Moon Lady* and telling her about my dreams. Jesus! I couldn't believe Susan would even think of that!

"Hey, I was just offering suggestions. Besides, some people that I have talked to told me that she is not a nutcase—at least not all the time. Some of the shit she has said has come true. She has been right a number of times. I'd try anything if I was going through the torment you are with that damned snake dream," she added, and I knew she was just thinking of my well-being.

"You'd do anything, huh?" I asked, "What if this crazy woman tells me to wear beads and amulets around my neck? What if she tells me to walk into a fucking snake pit and wash away my fear in snake venom? What if she asks me to do some other God-forsaken stupid thing? Then the joke's on me and you guys can tell everybody 'get a load of Sandy, she fell for *The Moon Lady's* mumbo-jumbo.' No thanks. I just won't fucking sleep. Besides, I don't confide in anybody that doesn't have a real name. Or won't tell it."

"I'm sure if you asked her, she would tell you her name," Randy stated.

I couldn't believe he was actually conspiring with Susan on this issue. Now, I really wasn't hungry. Not even for that steak dinner I was craving earlier. When backed against the wall by those you care about, I have learned from experience, it is best to walk away and be accused of dodging the situation than remaining for a fight to ensue. Therefore, I got up from the table and walked out to Amaretto's foredeck. It was nearing late afternoon and the temperature was hovering near eighty-five. If it weren't for the low humidity and lack of mosquitoes, it could be any August day. But the sun was casting harsh shadows on the water, typical of late autumn. I stood on deck for a long time thinking. Not only of *The Moon Lady* and the way my friends thought I would actually talk with her, but of *The Dream*, Pudge, and how I wanted to go back to yesterday and start over again with none of this happening. Of course, it wouldn't take away *The Dream*, but that I could live with if there weren't anything else falling apart.

A long breeze swept over me from the southeast. It was warm and salty, and it held me captive while the thoughts slowly blew away. And then I thought of my father. Not the excuse of a father that just died, but Alex Darnell, the man whom I admired most in life. He came into my life when I was still running from demons, and he married my mother who I thought would never remarry after the disaster she suffered with Carlo. But marry she did, and the two of them were warm and loving toward each other until he died last year. He had been a man of the sea, and I never missed the opportunity for a yarn about the open water. We would talk often of ports of call and running where the ocean led. He met Pudge only once when Pudge needed a strong back to help pull in nets during a heavy season. And we would spend our time together fishing from bridges or out on party boats. But, all good things come to an end, and so did mine. He died unexpectedly, leaving me without a father and mom without her love. So, off to Europe she went after six months, intent on spending part of her remaining years soaking up the sun on the French Riviera.

I suppose I had always been somewhat of a failure to her, never settling down as my sister did and always opening my mouth when I had nothing nice to say. I remember well the day I told her I was having a baby. She nearly died. Especially when I told her I had no idea who the child's father was. It was my dad who saved me and Shane. And I suppose the whole thing turned out well in the end, but now I really missed him. I missed not having him here to talk with, especially now when I wanted so badly to find out what happened to Pudge. I found my mind turning toward Pudge and getting angry with him for not leaving me more of a clue. If he had decided to kill himself, which I really doubted, why didn't he leave a note? I thought if I were going to do away with myself, I probably would leave no more of a trace of my unhappiness and pain than Pudge did. Maybe he did kill himself, like the cops said. Maybe I was grabbing at straws in hopes that he would not have left me with such a large hole in my heart. I listened to the water gently slap against Amaretto and heard her bilges start again. It was soothing and disturbing at the same time. And it was time to get ready to go to Key West. I really didn't know what I would say to Steve when we found him. I was afraid I might kill him just because I thought he was the one who killed Pudge. I decided to eat the sandwich and went below to get it, saying nothing to Susan and Randy.

Chapter 3

No Name Bar, The Moon Lady, and another death

We were past the Seven Mile Bridge before I decided to speak again. When I get pissed, I find silence is the best way to convey my message. I don't have to get raving mad and start screaming. All I have to do is throw my "look" toward the victim, or in this case, victims. But my silent rage ended on the bridge.

"You have any plans when we find Steve?" I asked Randy as he piloted my van toward our destination.

"No, although I have tossed about several statements and accusations that ranged from 'listen asshole' to 'come, let's go for a little walk,'" he replied giving me indication that he was somewhat convinced that Steve had something to do with Pudge's violent end.

Susan chimed in with, "I don't want you two getting all geared up for a fight. I don't want to be the one who has to patch two hotheads back together. You don't know what kind of, or how many, friends he has in Key West."

I seriously doubted Steve had any friends anywhere and said as much.

With the tension broken, the trip began to take the atmosphere of trips past. The three of us staked out too many trips to the Keys to count not only memorizing every niche in the road, but all the surrounding waterways as well, especially since we began helping Pudge.

When we first met, I thought he was only after fish, but quickly learned that Amaretto was not only a fishing vessel, but a lobster boat and shrimper as well.

"I can change her to whatever I need her to be," he said. "Much like you. I thought you only wrote books, then I see you writing stories about old fishermen in magazines. Hell, I didn't know you could write truth, too."

Touché.

We decided that Amaretto was the perfect vehicle for one big bang of a trip to the Bahamas, and Pudge, Randy, Sue, and I spent a relaxing month exploring the waters off the Bahamas. We caught a few raised eyebrows from the upper echelon Sea Ray yachters, especially when we moored next to two investment banker families complete with snot-nosed kids and dogs. It seems we tarnished their expensive neighborhood with the likes of Amaretto and her stinking fishnets and her constant purges of yellow bilge water. But, we had fun. And we laughed and drank and dove until it was time to come home.

As the van neared Big Pine Key, we decided to go to the No Name Bar on No Name Key for something to eat. I locked my eyes on Sue and dared her with my best steely gaze to mention *The Moon Lady*. I turned my sights on Randy and made the point to him as well, just for insurance.

We pulled up to the bar and quickly ambled out of the van. We entered the darkened oasis and stood a minute to regain our eyesight from the bright sun to near darkness of dark walls peppered with one-dollar bills. We blindly groped our way back to the pier and opted to sit near the window when we passed her. *The Moon Lady* sans turban. She had platinum blonde hair stuck in an unnatural web of curls piled on top of her round head. Hair of that color should be outlawed, I thought. Her bright green eyes looked through me, then Sue, then Randy, as she carried herself past us to her table and self-proclaimed throne. It was the first time I had ever seen her without her turban and couldn't remember if I had noticed her hair color before, but I thought if I had seen it I surely would have remembered it. Her signature muumuu covered her ample round body from cleavage to mid-calf. There her well-endowed calf tapered to the thinnest ankle that could possibly be responsible for the task of holding up the rest of her. She plopped down in her assigned seat and drank from a tall glass of vodka and ice. She was bedecked with baubles, beads, and rings on every finger, looking like a gaudy Christmas tree on display in a store window.

There were perhaps ten other people in the bar including the bartender. All of them looked like local types in shorts, T-shirts, and sandals. Most of them had stringy hair laden with salt surrounding fine-lined sun-drenched faces. *The Moon Lady's* face puffed out any signs of lines, and her complexion was translucent white. She had enough makeup on her eyes for all the inhabitants put together.

We took our seats, and I, being most unlucky, had the dubious honor of sitting with my back to the setting sun and facing *The Moon Lady's* table. From the other side of the bar, a young man appeared and glided to her table. He looked to be in his late teens, with a mop of black curls that hung down to his shoulders. He looked at me for perhaps a second and our eyes locked. They were of the bluest blue and beamed at me a message I understood; I knew those eyes, but couldn't remember from where. I squinted at him and nodded in recognition, even though I had no idea who he was. He turned his back to me and sat with *The Moon Lady*.

Where had I seen those eyes before, I wondered, and spoke the hushed question to Randy and Sue. They looked at him and neither could figure out who he was.

"So," Sue began, "are you going to ask her about your dream?"

"Not today. I really don't think so," I began. "I don't trust anybody with hair that color."

Randy laughed and Sue joined in.

"I've never seen hair that color before in my life," Sue acknowledged, "and I used to work in a salon."

We made small talk among ourselves, but I must admit, I couldn't keep my eyes off *The Moon Lady* and her young male companion. The thought of those eyes would haunt me until I figured out where I had seen them before. Soon they were joined by a third person— a young woman. She sat opposite *The Moon Lady* and hung low over the table. As if taking a cue, the man stood up and glided back through the door leading behind the bar. *The Moon Lady* reached into her muumuu for her tarot cards and began telling the woman's fortune.

I couldn't resist.

"Oh, great one, tell me what the future holds," I murmured out loud in a joking fashion.

Susan tried to hush me, but it was too late. *The Moon Lady* lifted her painted eyes to me.

"You have little faith," she spat my way.

"I have great faith, but not in charlatans," I responded.

"You have great pains and masquerade that all is well. Why, you are looking for answers that you will never find. Mark my words, the one you seek is silent," she spoke the words like a true prophet.

"Answers? I don't even know the questions, Lady. And a silent speaker is the best kind," I felt compelled to get in the last word.

"You will see," she responded and cut off the conversation refusing to let me have the final say.

Before the verbal spar escalated, Randy made the sign that we should be on our way. He blamed it on the dying sunlight.

On the road to Key West, we chuckled about *The Moon Lady* and her "oh, ye of little faith spiel" and the way her words fell from bright red lips, and the remainder of the trip was quite relaxing.

Randy pulled the van up to the harbor. He instructed Sue and me to wait for him, while he inquired where we might locate Steve. He returned with the address of a rooming house near Duval Street, and we rode slowly to the location, fighting the evening traffic of tourists and local hawkers packing the narrow streets.

We parked and crept out into the thick night air, making our way to his room. The door was cracked, and two men, who looked like they had been on the water most of the day, quickly answered our gentle rap on the door.

"Is Steve here?" Randy asked.

"No. He's gone," answered one of the men.

"When do you expect him back?" I asked.

"I don't. He's dead."

For some reason, I felt the blood in my veins turn to ice. Randy is the one who remained calm enough to ask the next question.

"What happened?"

"Knife fight with a local kid over a poker game. Happened last week."

"Well, thanks for your time," Randy concluded, and we walked out in silence.

It wasn't until we were back in the night air that Randy grabbed Sue and me and said, "I think I need a drink."

We should have been surprised since Randy quit drinking, but under the circumstances, we could allow him a night or two of relapse. In fact, we could easily grant him a pass for endless drunken stupor after what we just went through.

I don't remember making it back to Amaretto. I don't think Susan or Randy remembers the trip either, but some things are better left unasked and unknown. If guardian angels do exist, - and I suspect they do, then I know three angels that put in overtime getting us back to the boat unharmed.

Somewhere in the fog, I remember having *The Dream*, but this time, *The Moon Lady* was there with her puffy face and red lips. I don't remember what relevance she had to the snake, but she was there. No doubt, laughing at me for mocking her like a high priestess without a coven. I said nothing to Susan and Randy about *The Dream*, and I don't think they were in any condition to have listened to my monotonous story anyway.

"Did you hear what she said?" Sue asked me as she sat on the foot of the bunk.

"What who said about what?" I retorted still in that foggy state of morning-after haze.

"What *The Moon Lady* said about the person you are looking for. She said that he would be silent. How did she know you were looking for someone, and how did she know he would be dead?"

"She took a stab and got it right. Besides, she said nothing about Steve being dead. She said silent as in mute," I said, trying to reason the usually reasonable Sue from *The Moon Lady's* spell.

"Well, you can't get more silent than dead," Randy interjected from the floor.

"What the fuck are you doing down there?" I asked

"I couldn't make it to the bunk. Now I know why I quit drinking."

"You really have to talk to Sue about *The Moon Lady*, Randy. Tell her that the fat old bitch is full of shit, will you?" I said. I was starting to get unnerved at Sue for hanging on the woman's words.

"Well, this time I rule in favor of Sue. Maybe *The Moon Lady* knows something we don't. And don't go sulking into one of your silent rages."

I got the feeling that this was going to turn into another shitty day. My head ached every time I tried to force it off the bunk. Just when I thought the silence was getting too unbearable and I was going to be blamed for it, Sue started reminiscing about some of our old drinking times. I listened to Randy and Sue banter about the time we all wound up beside the road throwing bait at the fish we couldn't catch. I started to laugh about it and eased their minds, I suppose, that I wasn't sinking into silence. Our brief memory was interrupted by a vaguely familiar voice calling from the dock. Randy got up from the floor and shuffled his rumpled body to see whom it was. He returned in a short time with *The Shark*, as we had taken to calling Mark Chaney. Funny, I thought, he began as *The Suit* and wound up as *The Shark*. No doubt, the three of us would wind up in hell when we died where we would be lined up against a hot wall as people strolled by calling us names like we called everybody on Earth.

"Mark, what a pleasant surprise," I said as I tried in vain to make myself seem less hung over than I really was.

Randy introduced him to Susan, and the four of us sat around the table that came to be known to us as "the place Pudge had died." He produced several papers for me to sign and turned over the box containing Pudge's remains. Randy tried to explain to Mark the strange circumstances of Pudge's death down to the last detail, including the demise of others and the missing box. He listened politely and gave wind that he thought we were making too much from a cut-and-dried suicide case. He added, if we needed any legal assistance, he would be happy to help. As he got up to leave, I followed him topside and walked him to his car.

"He left you quite a bit of money," he said.

"I didn't know he had a lot of money. I thought all he had was Amaretto and a little savings," I replied.

"Sometimes people do things like that," he continued. "Leave people all their money. But for some reason, I can tell it doesn't mean that much to you. You are having a hard time dealing with his passing."

If he *only* knew how hard a time I was having, I thought.

"Well, good luck, and remember if you need me, I am close by," he said as he got into his car and left.

I went back to Amaretto and collected some of Pudge's journals to try to piece together the magnificent life of a wonderful friend. I wanted to take them back to *The Hole* so I could ponder them and look for clues. I set Pudge's remains on the bunk, and the three of us cleaned up Amaretto before we closed her up and left word with the other shrimpers to keep an eye on her.

We piled our sorry, and very hung over, bodies into the van and headed back to the mainland.

When we arrived at *The Hole*, Mickey was guarding a box that had arrived express from Clancy. I took the package inside and opened it. My mind had changed gears from trying to find the clues to Pudge's death and the link to the other deaths, to where many of my family's heirlooms had gone, and the last time I had recalled seeing them.

Opening the box, I set a note from Clancy aside without reading it and found, to my utter horror, that not only was Jack a child abuser, but he was one hell of a crafty thief as well. I found several pieces of jewelry that belonged to my mother. As I recalled, she used to leave these particular pieces on her dresser. What a convenient place for a thief to lift them. I also found pieces of crystal that mysteriously disappeared from the house during my childhood. At least one brought back the painful memory of my being accused of breaking a cobalt crystal fruit bowl and discarding the pieces to avoid the blame. And here was the bowl, intact, in the box. I even unearthed some of my earliest manuscripts and letters. I couldn't believe what I was uncovering! Of all the nerve, this son of a bitch had. It wasn't enough to terrorize me as a child with physical abuse, but to steal into the deepest reaches of my soul and take my words! I hated him and was glad he was dead.

"What are you going to do with all the stuff that he stole?" Susan asked.

"I should throw it all away to protect my mother. All this stuff has been forgotten, and for me to bring it up now would only make her feel guilty about the other people she accused of taking them," I replied, convincing myself that was what I would do.

"Here, why don't you read the letter she enclosed," Susan said as she handed me the unopened letter.

"Because, I really don't give a shit what she has to say," I replied and ripped the envelope into six ragged pieces. I threw the pieces into the box and piled everything else except the manuscripts inside before sealing it up and setting it outside to take to the dump on my next trip there.

Sue got up and went to the kitchen with the intention of getting a meal together, but found I had almost no food to scrounge a meal from. She decided to take a trip to the store, and I gave her my Visa card and told her to buy whatever she thought I needed. I repaired to my inner sanctum and took a long shower and tried to rest. It didn't work.

"Randy had set himself up in the yard under the sea grape tree with one of Pudge's journals. As I approached, he peered over the top of the volume and squinted.

"He was a stickler for details. Some of these stories are really funny," he said.

"I know, I read a few. It was funny to read what he wrote about us," I said as I took a seat on the grass.

"What gives?" he asked, "Something's got you in knots and it isn't just Pudge. Is it the box?"

"Maybe a small part, but I still believe Jack, Carlo, and Pudge are linked," I replied.

"And Steve?" Randy asked.

"Maybe, but he could have just been killed like we would have liked to have killed him on any number of occasions. The others … the accidents, and then Pudge after they were gone. Like he was doing me a big favor or something. Christ, I have no idea where all of this is going."

I held my arms up to the sky, half to stretch and half to pull an answer from thin air. I was truly baffled and I hated the feeling.

"What do you want to do?" Randy asked. "You want to go on the road and see if we can dig something up?"

It was the first time the thought had occurred to me. Why couldn't we? Why shouldn't we? My interest was piqued and my eyebrows rose in wonder and interest. Randy could see my interest and played on it.

"I could use a trip," he said, "It has been a long time since I saw a change of scenery."

"Hold it," I said. "I may want to get to the bottom of all this, but this is November. And we both know I don't leave the tropics in the winter. We will have to wait until spring at least. That would give us time to plan. And it would give the cops in faraway places a chance to forget the accidents so when we show up to see the files, we are not suspected of being involved."

I was scared to death I would be framed for this shit, and I had no intention of trying to explain that, yes, I hated Carlo and Jack, but no, I didn't pay to have them killed, and I didn't drive them off their respective roads at the same time. For some reason, I couldn't help but think that I was being watched by someone to see how I would handle this whole blessed mess. And, as I explained to Randy, my Italian Catholic upbringing had already steeped me in the *guilt without sex* syndrome so long that I was guilty by suspicion even if I had been on Mars when all the things happened. Randy took the time to explain that Jack and Carlo died at almost the same time, and it would have been impossible for me to have killed them both anyway. Notwithstanding, I pointed out, I could have had it done. He explained that I was too busy working and probably was too drunk to have been able to do any major planning. I grinned. He knew me even better than I knew myself sometimes.

That evening, after a fine meal courtesy of Susan, we began making our plans for a trip to north Georgia and New Jersey in March. I wanted to wait until there was no chance of bitter cold weather. Susan wanted to leave in the cold of January and Randy mediated that March sounded like the great compromise. We would drive the van and take our time collecting police reports and interviewing as many people as possible that were connected to the two. And on a very upbeat and secure note, the evening ended with Susan and Randy leaving for home and me settling into the silence of *The Hole* to return to my nocturnal writing and reading. Alone in my peace and surrounded by the quiet only a tropical Florida autumn night can provide.

For some time, I put off reading the journals, but after a while, I decided to delve into the private mind of Pudge. My eyes crept over the words, and on several occasions, I found them moistened by his revelations and descriptions. My body ached to be on the open water again, and it was as if Pudge knew that and wrote these words for me. He called me, more than a couple of times, his most trusted and valued friend. Those words hung over me like a shield, and I felt the warmth of his embrace as if he were in the room with me. Several times, I found his references to certain people entertaining. He had the same knack that Randy, Sue, and I had for labeling people, especially those he disliked. Among them, his ex-wife, alias Her Royal Cold*nass*; his daughters, Useless and Even More Useless; Josephine, (the woman most often mentioned in times of tenderness) The Gypsy; Josephine's son, and I assume Pudge's, too, The Gypsy Boy. There were also several names for Steve the Slime, alias Shithead, Druggie, and Asshole. I was called the Cynic—wonder where he got that; Randy was Stretch; and Susan was Princess. I also found a reference to the Shark— in Pudge's words: "How could I not trust an attorney who thinks so little of his profession that he hung the shark outside his office?"

What a piece of work my dear friend was.

Chapter 4

Springtime

I ask myself, year after year, in that same childlike wonder, why in the hell the months between November and March seem to stretch for an eternity. After thirty-six years, I still haven't found an answer other than I despised winter more than cottage cheese, if that could be possible. The reason, I surmised, was that being born in New Jersey, to a working-stiff family that could ill afford the niceties of heated driveways and long winter vacations, made winter without hibernation a fact of life. And when you have winter upon winter upon winter when you are a summer-at-the-beach person, it does something to your mind. I well understand why suicide rates climb in December; notwithstanding all the bullshit associated with the holidays. Summer people kill themselves in winter because the sun is so far away and warmth grows so distant that the mind's eye loses sight of reality. This holds true, a scientific experiment, even when the subject has been removed from New Jersey winters for more than half the subject's life. Even without the dreaded cold, and, gasp, snow, the subject's mind still views the long shadows and crisp air with disdain, even if the cool air hovers on the average of seventy degrees. Hell, seventy degrees to a ninety-degree person might as well be zip. So, I'm fucked up. What else is new?

I spent the majority of the past few months in hibernation either deep within the bowels of *The Hole* or on Amaretto. I did write a few noteworthy pieces that pleased my agent and padded my bank account, but nothing earthshattering. I took a small business trip to Los Angeles and was gone for two days when I got a nosebleed and told my agent to go screw. I hated California and the dry weather, too. San Francisco I could tolerate with its misty mornings, but not Los Angeles. I realized long ago when I lived in Los Angeles that every strange person in this world that I was not related to lived there. Could there be any hope for a Floridian who hated every place else, I wondered? Nope. Nothing compares to a moist subtropical summer. And the humidity prevents nosebleeds.

Also during the winter, Randy and Sue decided to sell their house. They had toyed with the idea of moving from the city of Homestead to the Redland to get away from the increasing restrictions of a city government not yet over its growing pains. It was a scant five years ago that the main store on Krome Avenue in the center of Homestead was home to a giant sign that screamed, "DEPARTAMENT STORE," for all to see. That was when Homestead was a place worth living in. It was quaint, quiet, and a little backward. Now it had grown— or so it thought. I found it all rather comical, myself, watching a small city try on big-city shoes. But I was used to the antics of Dade County government— in itself no great prize— which always kept me amused. So Randy and Sue decided to take the plunge after getting fined for leaving their trash can out longer than the allotted period of time. They sold their home.

They didn't have another in mind when it sold, but they had an idea. Sometimes, ideas can be as good as the real thing. In December, they moved into *The Hole* with me until they could find another house.

In December, something else of note happened. Shane's girlfriend took a spill during, of all the stupid things, cheerleading practice, and lost not only her contention for the squad, but the baby. Shane was crushed. Shannon blamed Shane and *his* baby for her unfortunate spill during practice and decided she wanted nothing else to do with him. Here he was, thinking about fatherhood and all the impending responsibility while she was thinking about the cheerleading squad. I was mortified, but bit my tongue—something I found I had grown rather good at with practice.

Shane moved back to *The Hole* and even agreed to follow the house rules:

1) This is my house, not yours— respect it;

2) No teenage congregations on my domain (you're lucky that you're allowed here);

3) Pay as you go— there is no free anything;

4) Clean up after yourself, as I am not the model housekeeper and will not change now;

5) Don't touch my things as they are mine and are not community property;

6) You are the kid, I am the mother and never the twain shall meet. In other words, what I say is the supreme law and you can't win;

7) If you bring another pony-tailed whiner into this house, I will go berserk and grab a gun. Don't tempt me;

8) Do your own laundry;;

9) Don't even think about quitting your job

10) I'm a bitch. I know it. Don't try to change things;

I don't know if he had contact with Shannon, but I know her father called me one evening and told me what a piss-poor excuse for a mother I was. I told him when he knew what it was like to be a single mother, or any kind of mother at all other than the type he was, to call back. For some strange reason, the thought of this "professional," as Shannon called him, in his suit, telling me what I did wrong or right in raising my son boiled my blood, especially after his daughter was more interested in the virtues of cheerleading than motherhood. I managed the last word by telling him that the reason he wore a suit and tie every day to work was to keep the foreskin from sliding over his head. Randy spit his dinner out and Susan had to leave the room when I said it, but I was backed in a corner.

I never heard from him again. I guess he quit wearing ties and couldn't talk. For eighteen years, I was the quiet mother type. I never interfered with my son's schooling. I kept my mouth shut when his school had great debates over the literary value of certain books and even baked cakes to raise money for their causes. I never had an unkind word to a teacher, administrator, or the parent of a friend, no matter what I thought. Now, he was on the brink of adulthood, and I saw no reason to take this abuse anymore. I was growing less tolerant of the world, and, as Randy so deftly put it one night, I was the only person who grew up in the 1960s that refused to give up the ship. I learned a lot and vowed never to change. The world around me may have endured the sweeping changes of the dead decade and the decade of greed, but I was still out in left field dancing to my own music and sticking to my convictions. The only thing I gave up was drugs. And that was because I couldn't find any good stuff around anymore. I sincerely believed everything was cranked out of some government garage or shipped into the country via the CIA, and I would not give the government any more money than it deserved, which was not much in my book. I didn't have to tell anybody how the government could fuck up. So I wasn't about to trust them as far as drugs went. I settled for Jamaican rum. For some time, I saw myself as the lone crusader in a world of misfits. I knew I couldn't recruit nonbelievers à la televangelists, so I figured I would just stay in *The Hole* and let the world pass me by. I had no desire to become a part of the competing workforce or a social climber. I would rather be left alone. True, I did take to Lee. I guess everybody needs love now and then, but when he left, I wasn't bitter. After the initial shock, I was rather relieved that I was alone again as if that was the way I was meant to be. Now, here I sit with Randy, Susan, and Shane around me, and I have become part of the largest anti-social dysfunctional family that could possibly exist. All we needed was a sprinkling of winos to loiter the property. No doubt, my neighbors, although obstructed from view, gossiped about what was happening at *The Hole*. Oh, I could imagine, "Dear ,come quick, that lunatic writer has more people living there! I feel sorry for her kid. Imagine growing up like that ..." I smiled in satisfaction. Keep 'em guessing, I thought. Don't say a word. Just smile and wave.

In February, we started planning our trip. Randy had compiled a list of all the stops we had to make and all the information we needed. I really felt uneasy about waltzing into unknown police stations to collect public records, but figured I could get away with sending Randy in to get that stuff while I pored over newspaper files. Because I knew of the immense paper trails that follow people, I have taken every precaution to eliminate my own. Susan and I joked about how I was quick to give out the wrong name when asked by strangers. That wasn't my only privacy quirk I had learned. Sue kept following me around saying, "See, that's another thing you do. You really are strange."

We decided that Susan's part in the whole trip would be one of great importance. She would be our southern spokesperson by virtue of her accent and looks. I never trusted backwoods rednecks in small southern towns, even though I was more southern than I cared to give credence to. Call it a throwback to when I was a little kid and my family moved from a northern city to a small southern outpost. Face it, it was no place to be in the early 1960s, especially if you happened to be Italian, Catholic, and didn't stand up for "Dixie." So I harbored a slight wariness to small southern towns with names like Milleville, Riverton, Aynor, Mullins, and Villa Rica, especially if the towns had population signs out front that boasted numbers in the two digits. Then I knew I was in trouble.

I had called my mother and told her about the quest we were to embark on, and she cautioned me.

"You know those people don't like others poking in their business," she warned.

"I know, but I have to do it. I think this is all tied in with Pudge."

"Well, I could never tell you what to do anyway," she continued, "just keep me posted on the dirt you dig up."

I felt like my mother knew something that I would unearth, but far be it from her to save me time and trouble by telling me anything. As always, everything in our family was a secret, and I was always the last to know. The only reason I found out was because some stranger said something to tip me off. Hell, the only way I found out my birth father was fucking the girls I went to school with was because he was the hit of junior prom gossip. I was a freshman at the time. He would invite these girls over and dick them right there in my own house! And then he became the topic of the punch bowl gang. No telling how many he screwed. In the end, a car screwed him. I half-expected it was one of his "girls" that ran him down in the end. But that wasn't the strangest secret in my family.

I can remember when I noticed that certain relatives looked amazingly like other relatives that they shouldn't. Like a cousin that looked an awful lot like an uncle. It ain't brain surgery, and it all fit neatly together: there were people screwing people that they shouldn't have been—nothing like saturating the gene pool of our family. Perhaps that was the reason that I only spoke with my mother, sister, and one or two cousins. The rest were good as gone. I had no idea where they were, even what their names were anymore, and I didn't care. It had become a game of names and faces over the past ten years, and I kept my distance. My mother's mother may have started the whole thing anyway with her husband pining for her older sister. That whole affair, although unconfirmed, gave birth to two lookalikes: my mother's sister and my great aunt's daughter. They looked more like sisters, and both resembled my grandfather too strongly for coincidence. But, be that as it may, everybody kept their dirty little secrets from me. They were scared of me, afraid I would write about it or something.

One day, my cousin Deana, the only one I speak with regularly, and I made a list of all the people in our family that we found were products of incest and/or misguided passion. We roared with laughter at some of our findings even though we were not unscathed by what we called "the Bartinelli curse." What we found even more interesting was that "the Anitello curse" was just as bad so that made me a two-time loser. Deana summed it up by saying, "If anyone in this world has a reason for being fucked in the head, you do, just by virtue of where you came from."

I agreed.

I had nothing better to do with my time between writing, than ponder my family. That made it worse for my relatives. My mother yielded several clues after thirty years of secrecy when she found I was her only friend in this polluted sperm soup of a family. My mom, my dad, who thankfully had a normal family as far as we knew, and I would talk for hours about it, and my dad would wrinkle his brow at her and say, "You wops are all screwed up. Never could stand Italians. No wonder Sandy changed her name." Ain't it the truth.

I amused Susan and Randy with some of the stories and decided to include Shane in the conversation because I was always denied these precious tidbits and saw no reason to continue the masquerade. Since he had no way of knowing what the paternal half of his genetic makeup consisted of, and neither did I, he could rest assured that he inherited the worst of all possibilities from me. He quickly became convinced that his ghost of a father's family could not be any weirder than mine. For his sake, I hoped he was right.

Chapter 5

The trip

The time to leave was nearing, and I decided I needed to take a trip to Amaretto just to make sure she was secured and to let the other guys know they had to keep an eye on her while I was gone. I stopped in to see Harve and to let him know that Shane would be staying at *The Hole*, and he knew how to contact me if there were any emergency. Harve assured me that Amaretto would be fine.

"She's a tough ol' bitch," he said. He apologized for what he said. He mumbled something about things changing so a man had to watch what he said lest he wind up in jail or something. I smiled to myself and didn't get into the debate with him.

I boarded Amaretto and got the strangest feeling like something was amiss although everything looked in perfect order. A chill swept over me freezing me in my tracks, and only my head moved to look all around me. Ordinarily, I could still hear the water slapping Amaretto's sides, but I could hear nothing except the short bursts of air escaping my nostrils. My ears ached from the silence, and I thought I'd gone deaf. As quickly as the chill came, it left, and I slowly stepped into Pudge's cabin. Finally, I could hear the birds and the water again and, thank God, the purge of the bilges, Amaretto, aye. I glanced at the brown container on the bunk and the old captain's hat next to it.

"Pudge," I said aloud, "I'm on my way. I'm going to find out what in the hell is going on."

It was then that I noticed that the box had been moved. Pudge's bunk was soft, and even the indentation of a finger stayed exactly in place until smoothed over deliberately. The corners of the box didn't line up within a half-inch. I spun around to look behind me, as I felt unusually paranoid. Someone had been here and messed with Pudge's remains. I didn't like it any more than I liked the feeling that was rushing over me.

"Harve!" I yelled as I bounded off Amaretto, "come here a minute."

"What is it?" he replied as he ambled closer to me.

"Have you or any of the other guys been on Amaretto?" I asked, and then realized it sounded as if I didn't want them there. He picked up on my tone and recoiled at the absurd question.

"Well ... I," he began cautiously.

"Look, I didn't mean that the way it came out. I don't care if you guys are on board Amaretto. She's as much yours as she is mine, and you know that. But I got this feeling when I was down there that something weird was happening," I said. I noticed his look softening and was thankful.

"You mean you was spooked?" he said as his eyes grew big.

"Oh, for Christ sake, Harve, I don't spook. No, just that something felt wrong. And Pudge's ashes were moved on his bunk. Did you move the box?"

"No way. I don't mess with the dead, Sandy. And I try not to mess with the alive either," he said, "but I know the feeling you got. I was on Amaretto to borrow some grease the other day, and this wind come a-rushin' through her bowels like none I ever seen or felt before. An' I wasn't even drinkin' at the time. I got the grease and high-tailed it outta there. I'm tellin' you, she's haunted."

His eyes got big and he kept looking from side to side like he was afraid the others would hear him and rib him for being afraid of something that he couldn't even describe.

"But you didn't touch the box?" I asked.

"No."

I began to get another chill—this one emanating from within. Someone had been on Amaretto; if it wasn't Harve, who could it be? And why would they be there? And what about the cold wind? Jeeze, I thought, I was beginning to sound like the fucking Moon Lady.

"Well, if you see anybody on Amaretto that shouldn't be, you make sure you call Shane, and he will contact me. Remember, I am only as far away as the next flight home," I said to Harve in the strongest, most unafraid voice I could muster. I did a fine job, too.

On my way back to *The Hole*, I stopped in to see *The Shark*. Someone had painted giant red-tipped white teeth on his sign. As I was looking at it, he came out of the office.

"Someone else has a sense of humor," he said, as he approached, "either that or they don't like the way I do business."

He was tanned and looked too muscular in his T-shirt and cutoffs.

"How have you been?" I asked. But it was evident he was doing fine. I still couldn't place him in Washington with all those frigging government people.

"Fine, Sandy. And you?"

"Pretty good, I suppose. The reason I dropped by is to let you know that I will be out of town for a while, probably no more than a month at the most, on business. My son, Shane, is staying at my house, so if you need to get in touch with me, just let him know, and he will relay the message," I said. I hoped I led him to believe that I was truly on a business venture and not poking around playing detective.

"Sure, thanks for letting me know," he bubbled.

He told me to make sure I stop in again to see him when I returned, and I promised I would.

I drove north on US1, and at the last minute, decided I would take the Card Sound route back to the mainland. It was a wise decision. I stopped at Alabama Jack's and had two beers and some of those delicious crab cakes I had been craving. It was quiet there this Friday, not at all like the crowded Sunday afternoons I was used to, but that was good. I wasn't in the mood for crowds, not that I really ever was. It's just that, at Alabama Jack's on a Sunday afternoon, after hearing the good music and downing a few beers, the crowd envelops around you, and you feel a part of it. But this was nice too. The quiet gave me time to think about Amaretto and the cold chill. It didn't take long for my thoughts to sway from Amaretto to the trip. I hadn't worked as a journalist for some time, and this was starting to feel like old times. Except, this time, I could take Susan and Randy along. And there were no deadlines and competition. In lieu of that, however, there was the unknown, and I wasn't too sure I wanted to venture into it. A sidebar to the unknown was the fact that I was grabbing at straws. I had no idea what I was looking for or hoped to accomplish. I asked myself how I got into this shit and why I kept doing this to myself, but it was no use. I was too fucking old to change.

My time for pondering and eating crab cakes at Alabama Jack's was too short, and I started back for the Redland and The Hole. I had driven my alternative means of transportation, my pickup truck, this day. I had left the van behind in case Randy or Susan had anything they wanted to cram inside early before the morning rush. Besides, I liked my truck. Randy asked me once why I didn't own a car, just the truck and the van, and I told him all cars looked the same to me these days. I remember going to the 1964 World's Fair in New York and seeing the *Cars of the Future* prototypes. They looked like eggs with their rounded bodies and glass. I never dreamed all the cars would actually look like that one day. But, they do. Until someone in the auto world makes a car in this country that looks like a car, I told Randy, I won't buy a car. I'll just drive a truck. I grinned at recalling when I purchased the truck.

"I want that truck," I told the salesperson.

"Well, Little Lady," he began, "I can show you something a little more your style ..."

He winked at me as he said that, and I got really pissed. I decided to end the shit right there and then.

"Look, Bucko," I said, "don't ever, ever, call me 'little lady' again. You don't know me well enough to assume I am a lady in the first place, and, in the second place, if I am little, I have no control over it just like you don't have any control over your fucking pot belly. How would you like it if I came in here and said, 'Hey, little short fat boy with the fake hair; you don't want that. Let me show you something that suits you better?' You don't even know what I want. I know what I want, and I came in here to get it. Now are you going to let me have it, or do I have to go somewhere else?"

God, how I hate assholes.

I did get my truck, however.

There was never any doubt in my mind that I would. My only regret was that asshole got a commission on the sale. I hope he remembered me when he got his paycheck that month.

I was nearing *The Hole* when I noticed the house next door had a sold sign above what seemed to be the forever FOR SALE sign. I think the house had been for sale for about a year. Randy and Susan toyed with the idea of buying the house, but set their sights on the one on the other side of *The Hole*; it was closer and smaller, more like them. We decided that as soon as we returned from our excursion, they would put a down payment on it with a little help from Pudge's money and me. I didn't relish the thought of having neighbors after being without them for so long, but there was enough insulation at *The Hole* to buffer any intrusion—almost. I say that only because the last residents had this bird. *The Squawking Bird*. They saw fit to house it outside where I could hear it constantly. The bird from hell sounded like a broken record. It would say the same phrase for forty-five minutes, and then start a second and say that for as long. I found myself wishing I had a sling shot and even thought about paying one of Shane's friends to execute the fucking thing. I figured it would make a great sandwich. The owners moved before I had my way with their beloved squawker. I really didn't care who moved in as long as they kept their distance and didn't have a bird.

I turned into the driveway and made my way up the coarse gravel toward my house. Susan was outside talking to a woman I had never seen before. She had parked where I usually parked the pickup, so I swung around and pulled beside it. I noticed her bumper sticker "Don't Presume I'm Straight." I figured she had an attitude and I liked that.

"Sandy, come here. Meet your new neighbor," Sue said as I exited the truck.

She stood next to a very tall, tanned woman in her twenties with long, perfect auburn locks that played in the sun. She had the most striking blue-green eyes and the type of body that petite women like myself dream of. I guessed she was close to six feet tall.

"Hi," she said in a sultry voice, "I'm your neighbor, Mara. I'm gay."

I stuck out my hand.

"I'm Sandy. I'm not. But, I'm a writer if that counts." What else was I supposed to say?

Mara threw back her head and shook her locks. She laughed out loud, revealed perfect teeth and quipped, "I can tell I like you already. I am not a crazy party-type, in case you're worried about excessive noise. I am out of town a lot as I am a model, but I hope we can at least have a respect for each other."

"Fair enough," I replied. "You don't have any birds, do you?"

Susan shot me that look.

"Ah, no. Can't stand the things," Mara quipped. I knew we would get along just fine.

I heard the phone and excused myself, leaving Susan and Mara alone. Together they looked like the perfect threat to all insecure women—two extremely personable and beautiful women. I felt so small and insignificant.

The phone stopped ringing by the time I entered the front door, and I took it as an omen that things on this trip were going to go as shitty as it seemed my whole life had gone to this point. But Shane had answered it, and he was taking his time talking to my mother. I grabbed a beer from the refrigerator and perched myself on a stool to patiently wait for the end of his conversation. He smiled that little kid smile when he handed me the phone, and for a fleeting moment, I remembered the first time I laid my eyes on his perfect form swathed in a blue hospital blanket. The only time I truly felt a consuming love, and I still hadn't lost it despite our parent-child spats.

"Hi, Mom," I greeted.

"You're really going to go through with this, aren't you? I can't believe it. Yes, I can. I know you. Just be careful, that's all," she said.

"I will, don't worry. I can't die until I have the answers I am after. Then I can drop dead and be contented that I know all I needed," I quipped.

"Don't get smart," she said. "Who is going to look after my house? Shane? Don't forget to tell him that the dust needs to be removed from the corners behind the doors."

My mother: World traveler and survivor, yet she worried about dust balls. I shook my head and rolled my eyes, but didn't tell her that I hadn't checked the dust balls since she first told me about them.

"I'll tell him, don't worry," I lied. I had no intention of telling Shane that there might be dust balls behind her doors. Besides, he wouldn't notice a dust ball if it was the size of a bowling ball and followed him around the house.

She wished me well and told me to keep in touch with her while I was gone. I assured her I would. As I hung up, I pondered the differences in us. There were plenty of similarities, but the differences were pronounced. She kept at least one rein on me at all times. I chose to let Shane go—even early at that. For some reason, I think it had to do with the whole bonding process. I never stopped when Shane was a baby. I kept going full steam accomplishing what I needed to in order to make a living. My mother took time out and let her world spin off its axis while I was a child so she could mold me. And I still turned out the way I did, and Shane turned out as good, if not better—so much for all those philosophical studies on childrearing. I guess psychotics are born and not made. I certainly knew at that moment that cynics were. So were cynic-psychotics. I fit both categories.

My analytical thoughts were interrupted by a dual distraction— Randy running through the house cursing Mickey Dog who had a pair of Randy's jeans in his mouth and Susan bounding in the front door eager to tell us all about the friend she just made. I hoped she didn't welcome Mara into my house too readily as Susan was aware that there were few things I valued as much as my privacy. I was delighted that she hadn't invited Mara over in the bedlam of the night-before-the-big-trip, but she did tell Shane that Mara might need a hand in moving her things around. She warned him to keep his hormones in check, as Mara was not going to change for the "right man" as many men are inclined to believe. I gave her a sharp look and put in my two cents.

"And women never think they can change gay men?" I asked.

"Well, sure they do. I wasn't implying that they didn't. I was merely stating the facts as they pertain to this particular situation."

We played verbal tag for a while and finally gave up when we noticed that Shane had tired of the whole conversation and disappeared to his room and his heavy metal music.

Randy, out of breath from his chase with Mickey, had retrieved his jeans and announced that, with the exception of the three remaining suitcases and the food, we were packed and ready. Warmth came over me. I felt like everything was in order, and the trip might even yield something good. A far cry from the cold feeling I had earlier when I thought it was all going to be shitty. After all, I told myself, all the demons that could possibly haunt me were dead. I smiled and gave myself the hardest mental pat on the back I could muster. It's not every day someone does you the favor of killing your enemies. Gee, I felt so smug at that moment. Susan and Randy decided to get an early night's rest and retired to their room. I looked around my house and realized I was not meant to live with this many people. I could do a very good job of cluttering my house by myself, but the addition of three more people only made my home more cluttered, and I found myself becoming defensive and territorial. So far I had said nothing to my friends and son about the feelings of encroachment and was damn proud of it, but I wondered just how long I could hold out. I couldn't wait until we returned, and I could get the house next door for Randy and Sue. Shane was another matter. I hoped he would move out again and leave me alone, but in the same breath, I hoped he wouldn't move too far. I wanted to see him once in a while, as long as he didn't pair up with another bimbo.

I poured myself a glass of Jamaican rum and carried it to my room. I could still hear Shane's music. It changed from the scream of heavy metal to the melodic mourns of country. He learned that from me, I guess. I changed into a long T-shirt and was drawn by the music to Shane's door. I knocked softly and he let me in.

"What's the problem?" he asked.

"No problem. Just the music. I decided to come talk for a minute and go over some last-minute details. That's all," I said in a hushed tone.

"I know," he said, "no parties, no drugs, and no fucking up. Don't worry, I won't hurt any of your precious personal artifacts, and I won't squander your money on anything other than what it is supposed to be spent on. And I'll check the dust balls at Grandma's."

I smiled. "How did you know about the dust balls? I didn't tell you."

"You didn't have to. I have known her all my life. Anyone who knows her all their life knows that there are dust balls to be concerned about. Grandpa used to tell me about her and the frigging dust balls," he said.

"Watch your mouth, kid. Especially when you are talking about you grandmother in front of your mother," I joked.

"And you," he slyly retorted, "watch your drinking in front of your impressionable son."

I hugged him hard and my grownup son stroked my hair and whispered, "Don't worry, I'll take care of it all for you; I owe you a lot. I know it wasn't easy—what you did for me—and I love you for it. Thanks."

I couldn't reply. I had never heard words like that from him before, and I realized at that moment that the threshold from child to adult had been crossed. He understood what I had to do and what I went through to do it. I was so touched words escaped me, and I was never at a loss for words. I promised myself that this small fragment of time would be frozen in my mind and heart forever. I would carry it until my death.

I went to my room and rested on the bed, but sleep evaded me as it always does when I really need it. I decided to make the most of it and packed several pads and pencils as well as a laptop computer. I figured I might as well take notes. I learned a long time ago that inspiration always strikes when there is nothing to document with. Some things do come with age, I told myself, like the ability to foretell what moods will happen.

Just before the sun came up, I found myself thinking about what I was about to do and nearly panicked. I didn't want to revisit the places I left behind and the memories those places were sure to awaken. The crypt housing those horrid memories was sealed for so long and all the pain neatly concealed that I was truly scared the trip would unlock a flood of horror that would turn me into an even stranger individual than I had already become. At least I could deal with being strange, but not that strange. I vowed that I could handle anything and all the shit that happened was in the past, and there was no way it could touch me.

I reached for the golden anchor around my neck and rubbed it between my fingers. Good luck.

The smell of coffee crept into my sleepless room, and I padded to the kitchen to see who had been the first to wake up. It was Susan.

"Here, you need this," she said and extended a mug of coffee in my direction. "You look like you haven't slept."

"I haven't," I replied, "so what else is new? I hope you or Randy drives first, or it will be a short trip because by the time we get to Fort Lauderdale, I'll be sleeping."

Susan smiled. She knew me so well.

It took us about two hours to get our final things together, and, with some last minute instructions to Shane, we were on our way.

I perched myself in the back of the van and looked out the window, saying nothing, just watching the sun rise higher in the spring sky. Sleep finally washed over me before we were twenty miles from *The Hole*. I missed my home already.

I woke about five hours later when the van stopped at a restaurant.

"I guess you guys were going to eat and leave me in here?" I quipped in a sleepy voice.

"Nah, we figured the heat would get you sooner or later," Randy said.

"Ready for some lunch?" Sue asked.

"How about breakfast? I haven't had breakfast yet," I answered.

"You know," Randy said in his best authoritative voice, "the last thing we need on this trip is for one of us to be on night time while the other two are on day time. You better figure out a way to shake the insomnia, or we will wind up doing nothing."

"Don't worry, Randy. In a day or two, I'll be fine. And I have Mr. Rum to help me sleep tonight," I said with a smile.

"By the end of this trip, we'll be drinking the rum and you'll be straight," he replied, then added, "If you don't drive us to drink, nothing will."

"Fuck you."

"Good reply," said Sue, "but here's one better: fuck the both of you. Now let's eat."

Nothing like being on the road with your friends, I thought as I stumbled out of the van and squinted into the afternoon sun. Even if they do piss you off once in a while.

When our meal was finished, we headed back up the interstate and vowed we wouldn't stop for the night until we crossed the state line into Georgia. I think everybody who lives in South Florida and travels north says the same thing and forgets how fucking long it takes to get out of Florida. On the way home, they forget how long the state is again. and when the "WELCOME TO FLORIDA" sign comes into view, their insides jump with the joy of being home only to discover that home may as well be two normal states away.

True to our steadfast vow, we didn't stop until we were in Georgia. There was little talk left in us as we entered the motel parking lot. We were equally grumpy and travel weary. In silent conversation, we let each other know that we were trying to hurry and get this whole thing over with, but nobody was going to be the first to admit it. We got one room and took showers before we went to the restaurant for dinner. We kept our dinner conversation to general small talk. Susan had amassed several travel brochures from the lobby to make it look like we were tourists.

"I just want it to look like we are just traveling around on vacation," she said.

"Susan, we aren't doing anything wrong," Randy said. "It's not like we're dealing dope or anything. We are just visiting a few local libraries in small towns. What is the big deal?"

"I don't know," she said, "I get the feeling that something bad is going to happen, that's all."

"Just what I need," I interrupted, "Another fortune teller who foresees trouble. We ain't doing anything wrong, Sue. If you want to go home, go. But if you are going to stay with us, then keep your soothsaying to yourself. I need answers, that's all. I need to find out what happened to Pudge."

"I don't see how finding out what happened to Carlo and Jack has anything to do with Pudge," she said.

"We'll never know until we check it out," said Randy. "Now, make the best of the trip and think about Pudge; that's all I ask.

"Okay. Okay," she said and waved her arms in the air.

We walked back to our room in the growing silence. The last thing I wanted was for the trip to start tension between the three of us. I only had Susan and Randy left as friends, and I wasn't about ready to lose them, too. I vowed to be on my best behavior and even went to sleep promptly.

The Dream interrupted my sleep not once, but three times that night, and I didn't say anything about it to Susan or Randy. In fact, the sleep that I did get refreshed me so it looked like I had my first good night's rest in a week. So, I played along.

"Holy shit," exclaimed Susan as she caught a glimpse of my rested face, "You look great!"

I was sitting at the table drinking coffee and reading the local paper. No doubt, she expected to find me still in bed.

"Well, you don't look that bad yourself," I retorted.

"You must have slept pretty good then," she said.

"Yup," I lied.

"Randy, come here. You gotta see this," Sue called.

"Why not notify the rest of the people in the motel, Sue?" I asked sarcastically.

She smiled.

"What happened to you?" Randy asked as he caught a glimpse of my refreshed morning face.

"Valium in the air conditioning, I think," I said, "Actually, before I went to sleep last night, I told myself that I would sleep and sleep good, dammit. And I did. But, I have to tell you something: Morning is overrated."

"Are we ready to hit the road, Morning Glory?" he asked.

"Not until after breakfast," I said. "This *is* a vacation, after all. And we are going to have fun."

I was getting so good at playing the game it was scary.

We drew straws for the next round of driving and Randy lost. We omitted him figuring he'd done penance by driving the entire state of Florida, so I just took to the wheel.

"Play fair and then change the rules?" Sue mumbled, "I mean, if we were going to draw straws, then we should stick to it."

I looked at Randy and pleaded with my eyes for him to reply.

"I am tired of fucking driving, that's why the rules changed," he so deftly replied.

"I just meant that we shouldn't draw straws. We should just volunteer," Sue said.

We all exchanged looks and laughed as we knew that if it came to volunteering, we'd be stuck here in Kingsland, Georgia beside Interstate 95 for the rest of our lives. The trip to Mill Cove was a lot more relaxed than yesterday's trip out of Florida. In all sincerity, I believed we were suffering from withdrawal. It was hard to leave the springtime weather in South Florida, and, at least for me, even harder to leave home. I hung up my wandering shoes a long time ago and planted myself firmly in the Redland. The only time wanderlust swept over me was when I was near the ocean. Then I had to leave just to get out on the open water. As long as I stayed on land, I was fine. No matter how much the three of us bitched about Homestead and South Florida in general, we would never leave. It was something we all longed for all our lives. It was home.

We arrived in Mill Cove slightly ahead of schedule and checked into the local motel. I picked up the local newspaper and was delighted to read the non-news. There was nothing happening in this entire section of the world according to the sources quoted in the paper. Not so off the mark, I told myself, there usually was nothing happening anywhere according to most newspapers, unless the publishers wanted something to happen.

Susan sprawled out on the bed and leafed through the phone book writing the addresses of points of interest—the library, a restaurant, and the sheriff's office. She was great in her role as mediator, and the motel desk clerk was cordial to her and her accent. Randy and I played mute and smiled so much our faces hurt.

"So, where do you want to go first?" Susan asked.

"I don't have any idea," I replied.

She flipped through her notes and squinted.

"How about Rock Ridge Road," she stated more than asked.

"What's there?"

"The address of one Carl Anitelli. At least according to the phone book," she said.

"You're great. That sounds like an Americanized version of Carlo's name," I said. I added it would be a great place to dig up Carlo or Carl or whatever.

Randy sat on the edge of the bed drinking a Coke. He swung around and looked at me.

"Do you want to do this?" he asked. I noticed a certain note of concern in his voice.

"Fuckin' a, I want to do this," I said. "Why, what's your problem?"

"Not what's *my* problem. The question is what's *your* problem? I mean he was your father and you want to go see his death place with a gross relish. You give me the creeps."

I was stunned.

"That person was never my father, Randy. More like a sperm donor. There is a whole world full of strangers out there and a lot of them get killed. Do you feel for them? For strangers that you don't even know? For names you never heard of? In places you never heard of? All of them are faceless, nameless pieces of flesh that you never knew. I never knew Carlo. He took off when I was a kid. When I tried to get to know him, I found I loathed everything he stood for. He was a son of a bitch. He never gave anything to anybody— he only took from people. He wasted people's lives for the good of his ego. He raped everything he could get his hands on and stole into the night. He was an asshole. Just a faceless, nameless piece of flesh that nobody knew. And you want me to feel bad? Christ, you sound like my sister."

"Excuse me," Sue interrupted, "but this is hardly the time to trample on perfectly good friendships. Sandy has her reasons and Randy has his questions, that's all. Let's not dig too deep inside each other here. Some things *are* personal."

She sounded like a grammar school teacher scolding her two students. Randy and I looked at each other and apologized. I didn't expect him to understand my feelings, and I couldn't understand his reasoning, but I knew it had something to do with something other than Carlo. I believed this whole trip down my memory lane was exposing skeletons from Randy's past.

We called it a draw and headed to Carlo's last address with Susan, the Mediator, at the wheel. She steered the van about four miles outside of Mill Cove into the heart of fertile farmland. The highway sliced the farms in half and it reminded me of the Redland, only hillier. I was getting homesick. There were a few houses dotting the landscape and several barns. Sue turned onto Rock Ridge Road, and there were brick entrance markers on either side of the road. "Peace Mill Estates" they said. Yep, I thought, real peaceful. Imagine being out in your front yard in this shithole town and getting hit by a passing vehicle. Real fucking peaceful. I typed my thoughts into my laptop as we neared the house marked one. Susan parked on the other side of the narrow road and we sat there in silence; the only sound was the clicking of the computer keys and the birds in the trees.

I stopped typing and forced my head to turn toward the house. It was modest, I would say, something that I couldn't equate with Carlo. He was an excess type of person, as I recalled. If someone had something big, he had to have something bigger. This house was like his atonement, and I began thinking that there was some mistake. He certainly couldn't have lived here in this modest neighborhood. But then, I didn't know too much about Mill Cove. This might have been the premiere neighborhood for all I knew. I gazed across the front lawn and my eyes came to rest by the edge of the driveway. There, apart from the pavement, was a triangular garden set off by interlocking stones. The garden was ablaze with azaleas.

There was a "FOR SALE" sign out front, and Sue jotted the number of the real estate company down.

"Do you want to get out?" she asked.

My eyes focused on a stain at the corner of the driveway and road.

"No. I don't want the neighbors to think something's up. Let's go back to the motel and call the agent selling it. We can get a legitimate look at the place that way," I said.

"Right," Randy answered. Then he gave me that Randy look and added, "You're feeling something, aren't you?"

I didn't answer, and I kept typing. When I looked at the screen and scrolled back, I read an accurate description of Peace Mill Estates followed by goddammit, goddammit, goddammit, about forty times over.

"Sue, go straight and see where this road leads," I requested. She obliged and we snaked past the several models of homes making up the neighborhood. Some were two-story homes with sprawling yards and circular driveways. Others were small with few amenities. All were brick and had wrought iron railings around the front porches. The perfect neighborhood to raise kids, it seemed. Not quite the perfect place to spend the waning years. But Carlo never banked on waning, probably. And soon these little kids would be in high school. I figured there was no place better suited for Carlo than a neighborhood filled with young southern belles on the verge of womanhood. How tempting. How sick. I knew the reason he moved here and was thankful, on behalf of all the little girls and their mothers, that he was dead.

We returned to our motel room, showered, changed, and went to dinner. We said very little during our meal and returned in near silence. I picked up my computer and began clicking in the flood of thoughts I was having without saying a word to Susan or Randy. They were on the other bed watching television. When I work, I become totally submerged in my words, and this time, the flood was rushing higher than normal. I blocked out everything— all sound and vision around me—to the point of not hearing Randy as he poured a glass of rum for me and set it on the nightstand.

"I said, you look like you could use this," he nearly shouted.

It jarred me back to the here and now, and I glanced up at him and then at the rum.

"Thanks. I suppose you're right. And I need to call Shane and find out how everything is back at *The Hole*," I said.

"Ask him if he made progress with Mara?" Sue said as a wicked smile crossed her face.

I shot her an affectionate bird and made the call. Shane and I spent about a half hour on the phone just bullshitting about things in general. Now that I think about it, I don't recall ever spending more than five seconds on the phone with him at any one time in his life. But here we were, like two old friends. And I had not been away a full three days yet. I was glad to hear that Mickey was doing well; he was probably happier that I wasn't there to forget about giving him water and forcing him to drink from the commode. Shane informed me that he had given Mara a hand with her moving and met her girlfriend, who, according to Shane, was just as beautiful as Mara. Then he told me they were planning a surprise for us on our return. I told him I hated surprises and not to knock out any walls or anything, and he laughed and told me that he would make sure it was a surprise that I liked. Shane also told me that my mother hadn't called, but he checked for dust balls anyway; he didn't find any. He told me that Mark Chaney called, but said it wasn't important that I call him back; he had forgotten when we were leaving.

Shane told me to give my love to Randy and Susan and then asked if he could borrow my pickup. I told him I would convey the warmth and yes he could. End of conversation.

By ten that evening, we were getting kind of stir crazy and went out to find the nightlife in Mill Cove, Georgia. Atlanta, it wasn't, but we made do by stopping at a bar called Pete's Place and shot pool with the locals for a while. It was nearing two when Randy mentioned Carlo's name to one of the boys in the bar. He said Carlo hadn't been in town too long, about six months, but already he made a name for himself.

Apparently by screwing the mayor's wife.

"Why you askin' 'bout him?" the redneck asked Randy.

"I'm an insurance investigator from Atlanta, and I was wondering if he had any relatives in town?" Randy lied. He was getting good at this. I guess he picked up his style from me.

"Nope. No relatives here that I know of, yet, anyway," the redneck said with a smile. Then he continued, "At least not unless Vera's got a loaf in the oven, if you know what I mean."

"Well, thanks pal. By the way, can I get your name, in case I need more information?" Randy asked.

Damn, he was good.

"Bobby Bufkin. Hey, my daddy might could help you some. He's the sheriff of Mill Cove," he said.

Oh, shit, I thought. Just what we needed—some backwoods hick sheriff to follow us around—especially after the lie about the insurance investigator bullshit. But Randy played it real cool.

"Thanks, Bobby, I'll let you know if I need any help," Randy said and returned to our pool game. He even bought Bobby and his friends a few beers to make it seem even friendlier.

When we returned to the motel, I got a shiver almost as severe as the one I had on Amaretto. My mind was chock full of 'what ifs,' and I couldn't help but think that something was going to fuck us up, and we would never get out of Mill Cove again. That would be news for their paper at least: "Strangers invade Mill Cove and get what's coming to them."

"You worry too much, Sandy," Randy said. "Bobby is harmless and so is his daddy; lighten up and have fun at this, will you?"

"Yeah," I said, "I'll give it a try."

I crawled into my bed and fell into a deep slumber.

It was dark and foggy as I walked toward Amaretto. I could barely make out the name on her stern. I pulled my coat up against the damp mist that was so thick, I couldn't even see my feet, and they felt as if they weren't walking on the dock at all, but only on the wings of the mist. As I neared Amaretto, I half-saw and half-sensed that Harve was nearby. His face took on the ghastly glow of yellow moonlight. He wasn't talking, just laughing and pointing to Amaretto. I floated over her side and across the deck to the cabin door. It opened before me, and there was Pudge motioning me to come inside. He looked different— eyes crazed under his cap and his skin ashen. He removed his hat and half his head with it. I gasped in horror and reached out to cover his wound, but my hand never reached him, or maybe it did, but it went through him. He smiled and pointed at the table covering the secret hold then motioned for me to move the table. I pushed the table away and looked at Pudge hovering over me. I reluctantly opened the hold and reached inside for The Box. Something grabbed my arm and jerked me hard to the floor. I held onto the table with my free hand and looked to Pudge for help, but he wasn't there. My face smashed against the floor, and I knew I couldn't keep myself above the hold, but I knew I couldn't fit below either. I opened my mouth to scream, but nothing came out. Squeezing my eyes closed and trying to free my arm became exhausting, and I felt myself panicking. As I opened my eyes, I saw *The Moon Lady* in Pudge's place chanting in some strange language. My shoulder fell below the floor and my face squeezed in after it. The hold was damp, dark, and cold. My legs and feet poured over the sides of the hold until I was completely enclosed below the surface of the floor. The thing that grabbed my arm came up slowly around my leg and pulled me down, down, down, into darkness. The taste of salt stung my lips, and I gasped for air and clawed at the phantom sides of the hold trying to pull myself up. From above came a radiant shaft, and it shone below me on something green and crystal—the emeralds. I couldn't reach them; they were too far away, and I couldn't pull myself up. With my last gasp of air, I let out a scream, "Pudge! Help me!"

"Jesus Christ, Sandy! You need help! Wake up!" Randy yelled as he shook me up and down on the bed. I sat upright on the flimsy mattress and wiped the sweat from my face.

"Sorry," I said staring at Randy and Susan. I was sure my eyes were about to bulge out of my head; I could feel them swell, and I tried to will them back to their normal size.

"Was it the Snake Dream?" Susan asked.

"Yes. Only different. Real scary, if you can believe it. Not disturbing, out and out scary," I confessed, then decided to add, "but nothing that I can't handle."

There, I felt myself gain control over the fear, and my eyes were getting back to their normal places in their sockets.

"All right, I've had enough of this bullshit," Randy said in an unusually perturbed voice, "when we get home, you are going to get help, if I have to fucking drag you to a doctor. This is getting crazy. You're starting to bother me."

I glared at him and tried to fight back the rage that was growing inside me.

"You think a doctor is going to stop these dreams? I go to some doctor and say, 'I'm having nightmares' and poof, like magic, they're gone? When this whole thing is over, *The Dream* will end. Just give me time, for crying out loud, Randy. I'm dealing with this the best way I know how," I shouted.

His look softened and he sat on the edge of my bed. He reached out and patted me on the shoulder like a father comforting a child. I recoiled.

"Look, I'm worried. The stress is getting to you. Try to relax and wipe your mind clear. I'm truly worried about you, that's all. Just take it easy," he softly said.

"Yeah, we're all in this together," Sue added.

"Yeah," I said, "Just the three of us. I'm okay now. I'm tired. I want to go to sleep."

I lay down and closed my eyes pretending I was falling asleep, but I didn't sleep the rest of the night. I just watched as the harsh streetlights faded on the curtains until they were replaced by the soft glow of the dawning sunlight. Then I closed my eyes and took an hour nap—a dreamless hour in the warm safety of the morning light.

I woke to the morning cartoon show that Susan had put on while Randy had gone out to find coffee.

"How you feeling?" she asked.

"Much better now that I had some rest," I replied.

She sensed that I really did not want to discuss last night, and I was happy that she didn't pry for more information. Randy returned, and we drank coffee and watched cartoons for a short time before Susan broke our diversion with a suggestion that she leave to get copies of some papers at city hall and the library.

Randy and I would pose as husband and wife and call the real estate agent to see the house that Carlo had lived in. Susan was really getting into this investigation shit, and she played it like a game. To me, it was digging up deep buried and forgotten memories that were better left in the mire of time, but she seemed to relish the diversion. Thankfully, she took control and I let her. Besides, I was no fool and was getting real tired of operating on little sleep and nightmares.

She left us without a word, and we realized that we were left without a vehicle. Not to be outdone, Randy jumped in and took over as lead person in this macabre play of my life and called a cab that would shuttle us to the real estate office in town.

After some quick pleasantries— half in a thick drawl that piqued my nerves to no end— we were on our way to visit Carlo's house. Mrs. Samms, the agent, talked constantly the whole time and finally turned into the drive. She was the type that asked questions never having any intention of letting the other person answer. Mostly, I blocked her out, but I could tell that Randy was fed up with not being able to say anything. As we stepped from her car, I swung around and faced the street. The stones that marked off the driveway garden were askew since we had seen them yesterday. I made a mental note and scanned the neighborhood to see if we were being followed. I found it quiet and serene, just like yesterday only without the chatter of children.

The house was bigger than I expected. From outside, it seemed a simple ranch style, but once inside, the walls broke free giving the aura of elegance. The foyer opened into a large living area and that melted into a large covered swimming pool. The tile was new, Mrs. Samms told us, as was the deep, plush carpeting in the bedrooms. And the kitchen was the latest in modern technology.

"Where is the owner?" Randy asked.

"In South Carolina," Mrs. Samms answered.

"Why did he or she leave such a beautiful house behind?" Randy prodded.

"Well, she had rented it to a friend, who lived here for about six months, and he left, transferred out of state," she lied.

"Well, it's very lovely," I said, changing the subject, "if you could give us some literature on the house, we'll get back to you by the end of the week."

We made some small talk with Mrs. Samms, and Randy played the part so well that I was sure he had her going. At least he could ask questions that I would never think of like: What is the median price for houses in this area? Are there any smaller developments? Any county restrictions on pets? and a host of others. Before we were done, He had me convinced we were considering buying a house in this part of the world.

We returned to the motel before Susan did and went over our information carefully. There was no owner listed on the house, and I thought for a minute we would have to spend another day in this place digging up legal descriptions of the house, but Randy— bless his heart—pulled the needed information from inside his jacket.

"Where did you get this?" I asked.

"From Mrs. Samms' desk. Didn't you pay attention when we were sitting there and she left for a minute to get me some information on the home before we left her office? Jesus, Sandy, you are losing it," he said.

The house was owned by Christine Malone of Marion, South Carolina. No doubt, our next stop.

"Did you notice anything different about the garden, Randy?" I asked.

"Like what?"

"Like the stones were different. I have a feeling we aren't alone on this trip."

"You're strange," he said.

"Thank you. And fuck you, too."

"Pleasure."

Susan came in on our game of one-upmanship, and she looked happy with her hunting expedition.

"You look like you made out well," Randy said, "either that or you met a nice southern gentleman."

"The last southern gentleman I knew left me stranded in Homestead, Florida," she said.

"Ahh, a fate worse than any I can think of," I piped in.

We all laughed and Susan produced several copies of documents copied from the court records. Things had gone so well, she said, that she had time to go by the library and get copies of the newspaper clippings of the stories about Carlo's death and the short, inconclusive investigation that followed.

"I guess they figured he committed suicide, too," I said sarcastically referring to Pudge's death investigation.

"Well, do you guys want to spend another night in this fleabag motel, or check out, drive for a while, and maybe spring for a really nice room at the Holiday Inn across the state line?" Randy asked.

We decided to pack up, drive for a while, get some dinner, and stop for the night in South Carolina. The following day, we could make it to Myrtle Beach and play tourists for a day or two— sort of the Floridian's Revenge.

It took us no time at all to leave the town of Mill Cove, Georgia with a solemn vow never to return to Mrs. Samms, the courthouse, Bobby Bufkin, his father the sheriff, or anything else, again. We made it to Charleston and somewhat civilization that night and stayed only one day before heading to Myrtle Beach, where, the three of us planned, we would rest for a day or two. We settled into a real hotel for the first time since our adventure began. We decided we had enough bunking together and sprang for a suite with two bedrooms, a living room, two bathrooms, a kitchen, and a balcony overlooking the beach. It was too cold for me to enjoy actually touching the water yet. Funny how Floridians are, I thought. Here we were, with an impressive suite overlooking the magnificent ocean that we all loved so much in the perfect springtime, and we were too cold to go anywhere near the water. We decided to do something about it; we scheduled a dive to test our nerve.

Of course, we stashed none of our own gear for the trip, so we had to rent everything, but we figured it would be great fun.

We nearly froze, and there was nothing to see. On the way back in, the captain asked us how we liked our dive, and we almost screamed, "You call that a dive? We call that torture!" but we told him we had a great time and then ran back to our room, ordered hot coffee, and took hot showers.

I called Shane to see how things were going at *The Hole* and was pleased that I still could not hear the chatter of voices in the background— my indications of party time at my house. He said that Mickey Dog really missed me and slept on my bed every night. I replied that Mickey was probably happy that I wasn't there to hog the bed. He had become very close friends with Mara already, and she was cooking for him almost every night. At least he wasn't alone, I thought. How funny, how we all have these maternal instincts, even if we don't have kids. Here was Mara, clearly with a hectic life of her own, taking care of my son for me. After thinking about it for a while, Mara was probably a lot better qualified to be a mother than I was, although I wasn't quite sure what the qualifications were. Shane didn't turn out too bad, I told myself. In fact, he turned out a whole bunch better than I expected since I was the least motherly person I could think of to be raising a kid in the first place. Sometimes, I wondered just who kept who out of trouble in the past eighteen years, Shane or me? When I finished my conversation with Shane, I lay on the bed and thought of possible excuses to leave on my own for a while. It had been years since I was here and there were some places I felt compelled to visit. As long as I was exploring the past, I might as well take a bath in some faded memories— good and bad. I hadn't told Susan and Randy about Marion yet, and I was wondering if I wanted to let them in on some dirty little secrets about that shithole. It harbored memories as putrid as Florence, South Carolina did for me, and the thought of having to actually set foot back there turned my stomach. But the beach held some good memories and I needed "good." My thoughts were interrupted by Randy's soft knock at the bedroom door.

"You up to dinner?" he asked.

"Sure. Randy, I have to take some time tomorrow and get out by myself," I heard myself saying.

"You think it's safe? I mean, with your thoughts of people following us and all, should we should split up?" Randy said with a tinge of true concern in his voice.

"I'm sure I'll be fine," I replied. "There are some things I want to check on. It's been years since I have been here, and there are some places I feel I need to go up around North Myrtle Beach."

"Well, if you think it's what you need to do, then do it," he said.

"Besides, it'll give you and Susan some time alone. I think you both need that after being almost attached to me since you both moved in, and especially, since this trip began," I added.

He smiled and shook his head. I got the feeling all was not well in the bedroom of Susan and Randy, and I felt strangely guilty about it as if I could go in there and coach them or something. What a dweeb I was at times. Damn my Catholic, guilt-ridden upbringing. In some way, I could find myself the culprit of any and every problem in the world if I gave myself enough time. Sometimes it took no time at all to blame myself for things.

Instead of the regular Myrtle Beach tourist fare, I suggested we drive north across the state line to a great restaurant called Calabash. There were few truly great experiences from my past that I could conjure at the drop of a hat, especially in South Carolina. One of the most memorable experiences revolved around the close proximity to Calabash in North Carolina, and the sensuous deviled crab on their menu makes the trip across the border worth it. This time I was afforded the luxury of driving and as I began to head up US 17 to North Carolina, familiarity swept over me for the first time since leaving my home state. I knew exactly where I was going and drove on impulse, conjuring the taste of deviled crab all the way to Calabash.

Being from South Florida and spending so much time in the Keys should teach me not to be shocked at the unbridled growth tourism spurs, but I almost missed the original Calabash. How the hell was I supposed to know that in twenty years, at least a hundred more restaurants would clog the coast with an array of signs so thick the Atlantic might as well be six miles further east.

Following one of the most memorable meals I had in a long time, we headed right back to our hotel. For some reason, Randy and Susan were getting quieter toward each other, and I tried to ignore it, but I knew if their silent little war persisted, I would eventually have to butt in and smack some heads together. This shit bothered me, especially since Randy was always torturing me with his notions that I should not be alone. One look at a marital spat and I loved my aloneness. Almost worshipped it.

Shortly after I closed my bedroom door, the phone rang. It was Shane. He passed on a message for me to call my mother. I glanced at the clock and calculated the time difference and wondered what was so important that it had her up this early. Worry began to consume me as I dialed the phone.

"Mom, what is it? Shane called and gave me the message," I said not even trying to conceal the sound of concern in my voice.

"How long before you get to New Jersey?" she asked.

"A couple more days, Mom. We haven't even finished up here. Why?"

"I was just wondering if you could check on something for me, that's all."

"It must be pretty important for you to think of it at this hour. What is it?"

"Do you remember John?" she asked.

John? John? Who the fuck is John? "Sorry, Mom. I can't think of John. Can you give me a little more to go on here?"

"You remember. He was the one that used to come over and visit when you were small. He did a lot to help us out around the house in Berkeley," she said in a way that made me think something was wrong with me for not remembering this person.

"Zilch, Mom. No recollection. I can't remember John. The only John I can remember was the John that Grandma knew, and I can't remember him doing anything nice for anyone."

"No. Not that John. John Zarelli. He owned a bar. You remember now?"

"Is this a game? I can't remember John. What is it that you want me to do?"

"I want you to call John when you get into Berkeley and tell him I didn't appreciate what he said about me when I got remarried."

My eyes were closed. My head was shaking. I couldn't believe I was having this weird conversation with my mother about a person I couldn't remember.

"Mom, call John and tell him what you think. I can't do that. I don't even remember the guy. What am I supposed to do in this situation? This is like me telling you to tell someone I know to go screw. I can't do this."

"I suppose you're right. Forget it," she said like she was getting pissed with me.

"Come on, Mom. Don't do this to me. If I could remember the person, I'd be more than happy to tell him that, but I can't remember him. Besides, I have a whole list of people I am going to give shit to when I get there. I am sure I can more than cover the John thing by telling other people off— people that I at least know."

"You don't have to get all huffy, Sandy. I was just asking a favor. That and I am planning to come home soon," she said.

"When?" I asked, avoiding the John issue.

"Hopefully, I can be back in a week or two, but nothing definite yet. I miss my home and I want to get back. France is nice, but I really should get back before summer. I want to go to New Jersey for a while and visit your sister."

"I'm looking forward to seeing her, too. But I would rather not have to go to New Jersey to see her," I replied.

"Well, everybody knows how you hate to leave Florida, Sandy. It doesn't take long to notice that you are stuck in your ways. In fact, the only other place I have no trouble placing you is some island somewhere, where it is even hotter than South Florida in summer," she said with a laugh.

She knew me too well. I thrived on the sweltering summer weather in Florida. When it got so hot that you swore if you heard one more person say, "Well, if it's not the heat, it's the humidity," that you would kill them, I basked in this weather. Humidity didn't bother me. Heat didn't bother me. Sun didn't bother me. Hell, even sticky, tropical rainy afternoons when steam hissed off the pavement didn't bother me. It rather soothed me. But, let the weather dip into the seventies, and I was a basket case; I couldn't get enough clothes on to stop from shivering.

"Mom, whatever you want to do is fine with me," I said.

"I know. Sometimes I have a hard time deciding what to do. But I really want to come back," she said. I could tell she was missing Alex.

"Well, you just let me know what time you need me to get you and I'll be there," I said.

"Okay, Sandy. I love you. And remember, if you can find John, tell him what I said."

"No problem. Love you. Bye."

"Good bye, Sandy."

I placed the receiver back in the cradle gently and stared out at the ocean. I missed my home, too. I missed Amaretto. I missed Pudge and Alex and wanted to see them both just one more time. And I missed my mother. I looked up from the horizon and silently asked whomever it was that was taking notes in the Great Beyond to keep her safe.

I turned out the lights to give me a better view of the sea. I thought about my sister. I missed her. Mom missed her, too, I could tell. Mary was so different from me. I suppose it was a great diversion for my mother to visit Mary. She was saner than I was and more normal. She had a husband and children who knew who their father was. And she had all the nice trimmings of a home: end tables that matched, no dust balls on the floor, and little flowered curtains adorning her windows. She had things that I always admired, but never had the domesticity to see in my own home. At least Mom had one good kid, although she lived closer to the less admirable of her two children. I was too street smart, crass, and independent. I was the counterweight to the older Mary, and I made no bones about thinking for and of myself. The way I had it figured was that if I didn't take care of me first, then nobody else would. Mary never thought of herself. If she did, she never let on about it. Her thoughts were for her family and everyone else in the world. She ranked last. Hard for me to tell if either of these schools of thought are right, but I know that my way is best for me— at least I lived this long. Logic in its purest sense guides me. Hope, prayer, and kind thoughts toward others guide my sister.

From the other bedroom, I could hear the muffled voices of my friends. I sat and contemplated the ocean until silence enveloped the room. Then I made my move. I knocked on the door.

"Can I come in?" I whispered.

"Sure," Randy answered.

I went in and Susan was not there.

"She's in the shower. You have some 'girl thing' to talk about, or you wanna talk to me?"

"Don't get your hopes up. What's happening with you two? This is no time for marital problems. I'll pack you both back to *The Hole* and continue this venture alone," I threatened.

"You haven't made a single decision since this show got on the road," my best friend snapped at me. It felt like a slap.

"Look, I'm not in the mood for this shit right now. Don't start any crap here. You know I can be real hard to get along with when

I'm pissed, and I'm heading in that direction. And you also know that you are not above my wrath. So don't push, Randy."

It was most unlike him to act this way. In fact, I stood there trying to remember ever having seen him this way and couldn't. Thinking while on my feet has always been one of my more admirable qualities, so I seized the opportunity to exercise my talent. I headed for the bathroom, knocked once and went in.

"Susan, me and Randy are going down to the beach for a minute. I have to talk to someone about this shit and he is dry."

"No problem, we have nothing planned," she answered politely.

I went back to the bedroom.

"Get your useless ass out of that bed and come with me before I kill you," I barked.

Randy followed. He could see in my eyes that I meant business and was not about to take any shit from anybody. We dashed out into the cool spring night and walked toward the beach. It was low tide and the beach was wide, cool, and empty. The sound soothed us both, and I plopped down on the sand and stared up at my friend. He sat beside me.

"So, what is it?" he asked.

"Funny you should ask. I was about to ask you the same thing. This is getting hard on all of us. Maybe we should abort this stupid goose chase and go home. I miss *The Hole* and Amaretto."

"Susan and I don't get along all the time. Most couples don't, but you wouldn't know that because every time you are part of a couple and the road gets rocky, you bail out. You have never worked out a problem. You have always run from them," he said.

"Run? Hardly. Walk is more like it. And I know that's the way I am, but I'm too old to change. Now what's the deal here?"

"Nothing. Things will be better tomorrow," he said and looked at his watch. "Change that to later today."

I sat there and focused somewhere off the coast where the starless sky and the ebony sea merged into one. I set myself at just that point and let my soul free. How I wanted to get out there and never turn back.

"You know, you still haven't answered me. What is the deal with you and Susan? I don't want to be the reason for anything going wrong with you two," I said from my stance on the edge of the horizon. My eyes never strayed.

"You aren't *the* problem. But you are *a* problem sometimes. What is it with you? Is this whole trip getting so painful for you that the automatic defense shield is going up? The only time I saw you genuinely happy since we began this trip was at the restaurant tonight. What gives?" Randy said with a slight air of concern in his voice.

"Of course, it's hard. I know what I have to do here and I know why. But there is so much I can't deal with, and the worst part of it is, we haven't even made it to Berkeley yet where the real painful shit happens," I paused a minute before collecting every ounce of courage.

"Randy, I made a decision. I want to stay here at the beach. We can travel an hour or so every day back to Marion and get what we need, but for some reason, I feel safer here. I don't want to stay in any more fleabag motels. And I don't want to wake up in Marion again—ever."

"Whatever you say, Sandy. You're the chief navigator. Just let me know what I can do. But I wish you'd give me a little more reason as to why you feel this way. I think I deserve some sort of explanation. Things keep changing, and you know I like things somewhat structured."

I thought carefully about what he said, and I never let my eyes stray from the horizon as I told him of my first encounter with this fucked-up state. It was Carlo's fault. He dragged Mom, Mary, and me to Florence when I was a kid. It was the wave of the future, he said. And we would be happy. That was in the early 1960s. Well, I couldn't think of a worse place to be a northern Italian Catholic who knew no difference between black and white and had never seen crosses ablaze before. It was tough in grammar school when the kids made fun of the way I talked, and the bus driver stopped the bus because I sat with my new best friend, Jelitha, in the second row. The driver made Jelitha get up and move to the back of the school bus and wouldn't let me go with her.

When I got home that day, I noticed these men digging in the ditch in the back of our yard. They were chained together at the legs and swung huge picks at the ground. I stopped at the door to the house and stared in wide-eyed wonder at the strangers until an arm quickly burst from the house and dragged me in. It was Mom pulling me to safety from the unknown and the never before seen reality of the South—chain gangs working in residential areas.

I recalled the day the church we attended burned down. Funny how it was next door to the Baptist church, and that one remained unscathed by the raging flames. Ours, with its gothic spires, was gutted and left in ruins. The words "Satan papal worshipers go home" scrawled on one charred wall and "you're next" over what remained of the entrance. To the innocent eyes of youth, this place called South Carolina was everything evil. We were not wanted here, and the locals made no bones about it. We were forever outsiders, and there was no way we would become insiders. We held different beliefs, values, and ways of life to those people. We were the threat of the future. Carlo kept telling us we'd adapt; it would take time. But the whole thing was a nightmare. And then the unspeakable happened: The fight for civil rights. It became unsafe for us to be where we were. And we fled, without Carlo. He stayed behind claiming it was his job that kept him there, but Mom knew. He already found someone else. Hell, he found a few someone elses. We were safely back in New Jersey, and he was conveniently starting another family in South Carolina. When he came home for visits, he slept with a neighbor's wife. I guess the twisted Southern Baptist religion he became fond of omitted the part about coveting thy neighbor's wife. What followed was a brutal divorce and the isolation that it brought with it. It wasn't like it is now. Back then, I explained to Randy, I was a marked kid and my mother, a marked woman. We were the "tainted." Even in the sanctuary of our home state, it was difficult. I was not looking forward to going there either, I told Randy. That harbored perhaps the most evil memory of all—Jack Truitt.

Randy sat and listened to my story intently picking up handfuls of soft, white sand and letting it sift between spread fingers. "But that is New Jersey and we aren't even there yet. So far you have explained only Florence. What about Marion? What happened in Marion?" he asked, sounding like a psychologist.

I looked at him strangely and he smiled and patted the sand.

"Pull up a beach and tell me about it," he said.

I explained that I had to find out what my real father was like. Jack had raped me, and I carried that shame with me until it was unbearable, I fled to the only place I thought I'd be safe, to Carlo. Talk about compounding problems. Marion was as bad in my early teens as Florence was in my youth. Only the wounds cut much deeper. I went to a school, a private, lily-white school, which was fully integrated, although they priced "undesirables" out of attendance. They didn't miss much because the education there leaned toward southern, white male bias. A strict conformity was the rule, and it was as if every person there was headed for a future at the Citadel for boys or Missy Mae's Lily-White Finishing School of Homemaking for girls. I was fucked there because I questioned everything. Hell, it was good enough for Socrates to question; I figured it would be good enough for me. It was there, in Marion, at the height of the Vietnam War, when people I knew in New Jersey kept arriving in boxes—I found out by mail—that I began to depend heavily on the only two outs I'd developed in Berkeley: drugs and writing.

The drugs numbed the pain, and the writing kept what little sanity I had anchored firmly on Earth. I rebelled in everything, especially my writing. Those sacred words I had inside me flowed onto paper every time I had a falling out at school, which was very often. One day a teacher, an English teacher of all things, found one of my essays and called it seditious. It was about a woman and a man groping for love in the turmoil of a riot-torn city. "Too graphic," she said, and confiscated it. I fled the scene trying to remember the words on the confiscated paper.

Carlo kept badgering me to conform, but I couldn't. I wouldn't give them the satisfaction. I was thrown out of school and fled to my sanctuary at the Beach every chance I had. Carlo was seeing this girl at the time, a pig-faced, fat bitch a few years older than I, Laura. She felt threatened by my presence, and she needled him constantly, making up lies about my sister, who wasn't even there, and me; she told *Carlo with the great Chamber of Commerce aspirations* that I would ruin him. He beat me severely one day, and I had this terrible déjà vu of Jack, so I ran to that forever bastion of security—the Beach.

There, I rented a cottage with about fifteen people—all refugees from the Old South. I had dropped out of school and worked at odd jobs to pay my share of the rent. It was fine for a while. *Pig-Face* wasn't around and Carlo left me alone. Then they got married, had a kid, and called me to babysit. I told them to fuck off. I had no time for their shitty, cranky kid. And I couldn't stand to look at them. That was the last time I spoke to either of them. But a girl I went to the private school with wound up knocked up by Carlo. And it became known that he was dipping his wick in at least seven other high school girls. Laura blamed me for Carlo's infidelities. I told her she was absolutely crazy, and the only female person in the county not screwing Carlo was me.

Ahh, the beach. North Myrtle Beach was an oasis in the vortex—artists milling about, musicians playing everywhere, and me writing. I couldn't afford to go back to school; I had to work. And without school, I couldn't go to college. I seriously doubted there was a liberal college in the entire state. So I packed up and left.

My mother married Alex and moved to Florida. I followed, found my own place, finished high school, and set out to seek my fortune. I traveled to New Orleans and then to Los Angeles picking up a few dollars here and there freelancing. When I got pregnant, I came back to Florida. For a while, I lived in Key West; I gave birth to Shane and worked at several newspapers before writing my first book. With the money from my book, I bought *The Hole* and went to college.

"That is the end of the torrid story of my confused life. See why I hate this place?" I asked.

Randy looked at me with caring eyes. I could see a hint of pity there and I began to burn inside. I didn't need anybody, especially my best friend, feeling sorry for me. He said nothing and turned his stare to my focal point out on the horizon. I glanced at my watch and realized it was nearing dawn. The breeze had picked up and there were a few people walking near the water's edge. They strolled along the beach awaiting the sunrise, and we hadn't slept. I lay back in the sand and it was warm under my back. As I fumbled to find a comfortable position in the sand, I noticed a lone figure walking from south to north along the beach. He possessed a fluid gait as if his feet hovered above the sand. I squinted to focus on him and caught the shag of black hair that fell around his shoulders. The wind picked up and played on his locks. He shook the hair from his eyes and looked my way. Our eyes locked and a rush of recognition washed over me. I nonchalantly reached for Randy's arm and squeezed.

"Look," I whispered, nodding my head in the walker's direction. "Where have we seen that person before?"

Randy squinted at the form. It was a moonless night and he had only the waning starlight to aid him.

"I don't know if we have seen him before," he answered.

"Look at his walk. It's as if he is walking on the air above the ground. That's what I recognize. That and the hair and eyes," I added, knowing that by now, his eyes were occluded, and his hair was barely visible.

"You're right. I do remember that walk. But, I can't remember from where," Randy said as he scratched his head.

"I told you we were being followed. Dammit, someone is tailing our trip," I said.

"Big deal. What are we doing that is so wrong?" Randy offered.

"Nothing," I shrugged and said. "But it is kind of creepy to know that someone you don't know is following you."

Randy smiled. "Would it make you feel better if you knew the person following you? Then you'd really be paranoid."

I laughed and eyed the horizon again. The soft muted purple of dawn was peeking over the edge of the water, and we sat there in silence as the sky lightened. I glanced at my friend, and he looked lost in distant thought. I wondered what he was thinking. As for me, I felt better having unloaded the story of the past on him, and the dawn brought with it a security, a security in knowing I would not have to sleep in the darkness and dream *The Dream* again. Uneasiness was still there in the fact that there was a person tailing us, but the most unpleasant part of it was, I knew this person and couldn't place him. I watched as the sun, a giant reddish-orange orb peeked over the water and slowly crept up the sky. When we were fully enveloped in daylight, I suggested we get back to our room. Randy figured Susan was wondering if we ran off without her, but when we arrived at the suite, she was still sound asleep.

"I could leave and she wouldn't notice," he said.

"Sure she would," I consoled. "Eventually."

I smiled and went into my room, still not tired. I picked up one of Pudge's journals and began reading until I finally dozed with the open journal falling over my chest.

Some hours later, in my deepest sleep, I felt a sharp tug at my leg. I wasn't dreaming, but the hold was the familiar pull of the damned purple snake. I shook my leg trying to free it, but it persisted—this time striking intermittently instead of constantly. I forced my dreamless eyes open and saw that Susan had a hold of my leg.

"Get up," she said with her hand still around my calf.

"I thought you were the snake," I mumbled.

"I've never been called that before. Although, I have been called a few other things. By you, in fact." She was cheerful this morning. It was a far cry from the silence of last night when things between her and Randy were teetering on the difficult. She sat on the edge of the bed.

"You guys were out all night, weren't you?"

"We sat on the beach and talked."

"I know. I looked out a couple of times and saw you. I was going to come down, but I thought it would be better to stay here.

I was tired, cranky, and suffering from PMS. The last thing you needed was a bitch by your side," she said.

I grinned. "Is that anything like an angel in my pocket?" We chuckled at the female humor.

"Randy is still sleeping. You want to go pig out on breakfast?" Susan asked.

"Why don't we just call and order everything we can up here?" I said. I really didn't feel like going out into the world before I had a shower and changed clothes.

"Sounds good. I'll take care of that while you wake up," she said.

I placed the journal on the nightstand and trudged on shaking legs to the bathroom. So far, I figured, I had maybe six full hours of sleep since we left home. I looked in the mirror and saw that it was beginning to show. Staring at my reflection, I told myself what a screwed up life I had, and it had been a wonder I survived it at all. It was even more of a wonder that I had these two friends left. Vanity crept over me, and I began to ponder the aging face staring at me.

"Fuck it," I said out loud and waved my hand at the reflection before turning my back to it. I took a long, hot shower. When I emerged from the bathroom, I could smell breakfast in the living room and I went out to find that Susan had indeed ordered just about everything she could think of. We sat down and began scarfing food like we hadn't eaten in days.

"I can't help it," she said, pushing her blonde hair away from her face. "When I get PMS, I get bitchy, then I eat—a lot."

"I noticed," I said as I helped myself to scrambled eggs and toast.

"Do you get PMS?" she asked.

"I was born with PMS," I snipped. "That's why I ain't got no friends."

She laughed and shoved a sausage link into her mouth.

"Should we save some for Randy?" I asked.

"Nah, he'll be sleeping all day, as long as he was up last night. He can't handle those all-nighters anymore."

Between the sausage links and the eggs, Susan asked what the game plan was for this area. I told her that I needed to get away by myself for an afternoon at least to ride around. Then we would head to Marion to do some digging. As usual, she would get the difficult task of the police station and the library while I tried to locate the owner of the house Carlo was renting. Partially through telling her the plans, I remembered *The Floater*—the man-boy, on the beach. I asked her if she remembered seeing anyone like that with his shaggy dark hair and that strange walk.

"Yes," she answered, "don't you remember? At No Name Pub on No Name Key. He was with *The Moon Lady.*"

Bingo! The memory came back. Had it been lighter out last night, I would have remembered his ice blue eyes. But, I still couldn't figure out why he was here.

"Maybe he's on vacation," Sue offered.

"I doubt it, Sue. If you lived in the Keys, would you come to Myrtle Beach on vacation?"

"I wouldn't come here if I wasn't on vacation," she said. "This has turned into a bigger tourist trap than the Miami Beach. It was nice a long time ago, but it resembles Miami Beach too much for my liking."

"There are few places left near any beach that haven't stooped to people on vacations," I said as I shoveled the last of my eggs in my mouth.

"Well, we could spend a vacation in a place like Mill Cove, you know," she said.

I almost choked on the eggs. Susan tried to talk me into letting her come along for the ride through North Myrtle Beach. I resisted until she said she would play invisible friend. She wouldn't talk and would even keep her breathing down to minimum, if I wanted; there was no way she would feel comfortable with me out there alone, especially with that strange floating person hovering about. I reluctantly agreed to let her tag along if she insisted, which she did, as long as we could leave Randy in bed to get some sleep. We left him a note and headed out of the hotel. The spring air was borderline crisp and warm, depending on the type of weather you were used to. I was getting homesick and decided it was crisp. Susan, although she was in Homestead a lot longer than she readily recalled, decided it was warm and told me that whenever the temperature dipped below eighty, I always said it was crisp. She was right. The sky was aquamarine blue with a few clouds straggling across it as if they were hurrying to get somewhere else. I watched them and thought how like them I was. I wanted nothing more than to get the hell away from here.

I drove to North Myrtle Beach along US 17 and slowed just long enough to see the old bungalow I used to call home. It had been refurbished into a "luxury cottage." My, my, how things do change. There wasn't luxury in this godforsaken state as far back as history was recorded. There was always "luxury with a catch," either whites only, Baptists only, or people with plantations only, and now, Canadian tourists with lots of money only. I got weary of the beach, believe it or not, and turned away to head to a place once called "Sugar Hill." A paper company owned this parcel of land, and they planted it with pine seedlings. The sand was pristine white and black-water pools of iron-laden water formed little dips in the sand. It was a fine place for sitting and thinking and taking the heat off a sweltering summer day.

There were condos there. The sight soured my stomach, and without saying a word to Susan, I turned the van around and headed back to home base. She said nothing and asked no questions.

As I pulled into the parking lot, I told her, "The tour is over. There is nothing left to see that is worth seeing."

She turned the corners of her mouth into a slight smile and still didn't say anything.

"And," I said, looking at her wryly, "it is now all right for you to resume speaking."

She let out a sigh and said, "Things never remain the same, do they? Someone always comes along and pulls the plug on the balloon, and all the air escapes with the memories."

As usual, she was right.

We went back to our suite, and Randy was half-asleep and bumping around.

"Sometimes, I wonder if it is a female thing with you two that makes you do these impulsive things," he said and then added, "but, I look at Sandy and dismiss it all because I can't figure out if she has any nurturing female qualities that would give her an excuse."

He was back to his usual self.

"What makes you say that?" Susan prodded.

"Well, she never cries, and she never lets a man take the upper hand," he said as if I wasn't there.

"Perhaps," said the invisible me, "it's because I have never met a man with the strength to match my own. And I also have better things to do with my time than compete with men over who is stronger when I know it's me."

Score one for the mountain of strength with the insides of Jell-O that have been poked so much, she has to keep turning down the temperature to re-gel, and in so doing, has turned into the Ice Queen.

It was still early enough for us to go to Marion and get some things accomplished. We decided we would all ride there and see what we could dig up in one afternoon. I grabbed an old "lucky" baseball cap and my dark glasses, and we headed to Marion.

The wheels of the van plodded over familiar ground, and I was caught in a vortex of memories at some of the things that haven't changed. The road was pretty straight and flat. Each bridge crossing a river gave view to moss-laden trees that took on an air of mystique. I wished, on several occasions, especially as we neared Marion, that I were in another time zone. The putrid smell of the paper mill, some twenty miles away, hung in the ever-warming afternoon air. This place always smelled like something rotten and that didn't change. Neither did Marion too much. There were a few added fast food places, but it was still Marion. No doubt about that. The railroad tracks still acted as the color barrier. Paved roads and houses were on one side, and dusty dirt roads and shacks on the other. What a way of life, in the town time forgot, I thought.

Marion had a small library, smaller than the one in Homestead. But at least in Homestead, books could be ordered from other locations. This place had newspapers, not on convenient microfilm, but stacked and yellowing in the corner. We started to dig and found several articles that contained Carlo's photo and Americanized name. I had no idea how long he lived here, but I figured it was quite a while by some of the articles I found. There were eight wedding engagements touting him as the lucky groom to be, but only one wedding announcement. I wondered if all these little high school honeys had been knocked up at the time of the announcements.

The wedding announcement was to *Pig-Face*. The article said she was the only daughter of a wealthy tobacco farmer. He was a sharecropper with no teeth, as I recall. There was the birth announcement of a daughter almost sixteen years ago and several press releases from the chamber of commerce heralding his many contributions to this beautiful town. Puking was not allowed in the library, so I fought to keep my souring breakfast down.

"He was a great man," Randy kidded.

"Truly a cataract in the eye of humanity," I spat.

"I could tell. Check out those shifty eyes. You inherited nothing from him," he said.

"Yes, I did," I said. "Anger."

"I think that is developed, not inherited," he argued.

"But it's there. And I won't ever forgive the bastard."

Abruptly, the stories about Carlo stopped, until his obituary. It said he had two daughters, Mary Monticello and Charlotte Tell. Charlotte Tell was still a resident of Marion, as was her mother, the widow Laura Tell. Boy, they Americanized Carlo's name even better.

We made as many copies of the clips as possible before the copy machine refused to belch out any more. We figured it was tired from overuse, and we started to write our notes on paper in little scribbles of information that only we could possibly understand. There were few things left to gather in the great Library of Marion, and we sat at a large wooden table with chairs better suited for elementary school children and discussed what to do next. It was nearing five and we were getting hungry. We decided to ask the prissy librarian, who kept eying us, about places to eat. Randy, mustering all his charm in one fell swoop, got the location of a restaurant while Susan thumbed through the Marion phone directory for the address of Christine Malone, owner of the house in Georgia. She jotted down the phone number along with the address and then checked on the addresses of Marion-renowned widow Laura and grief-stricken Charlotte Tell. She found them both. I was glad. We could leave soon.

"Maybe while we're here, we can stop by the sheriff's office so I can go in and see what information they have there," Susan said. "This way, we can get the hell out of here. I can tell this place makes you shaky."

"We'll have to come back anyway, Sue. We need to get to the clerk's office and find out about property," I responded, thinking that we could do that on our way out of this state.

"Oh, and anything filed regarding his estate," Sue threw in. "Wouldn't it be interesting if he left something to that Malone person?"

I couldn't help but believe that Susan found all this interesting enough to want to dig for more. I had had quite enough of all this and was getting weary and homesick. I wanted to find out what happened to Pudge. I really didn't care about what happened to Carl, or Carlo, or whatever he called himself. And I cared even less about Jack. I wanted to go home. The only thing these people had in common, I resolved, was that they died around the same time— two by vehicle and one by gunshot. I was even more interested in finding out what happened to the treasure Pudge and I hid on Amaretto and why *The Floater* was following us. I didn't have enough time to sort out my thoughts before Randy said, "Let's get out of here."

We left and swung by the Marion Sheriff's Department. Susan went inside while Randy and I sorted out papers into a neat stack.

"You know, you're going to have to make some sort of list from all this shit. You haven't started to write anything that I know of yet," he said.

"How wrong you are," I responded. "I have been entering all kinds of stuff into the laptop, and I plan on sending it home tonight. I'll call Shane and tell him how to catch it all on disk. But, I haven't made any notes on paper yet. I will do that later, when I have some rum to clear the webs from my mind."

"I think you have a drinking problem," my friend offered.

I looked at him quizzically. "My dear Randy, I have a drinking problem, a dreaming problem, a man problem, and anything else you might dream up. According to you, I have very little time left remaining in my life and I am wasting it all alone. I wish you'd worry about someone else for a while. I am tired of you always telling me what problems I have and how to remedy them. This from a man who thinks tits are worth breaking up a relationship," I said with a smug smile.

"You don't ever forget anything, do you?" he said.

"Believe me, I try," I said as Susan opened the door and got in.

"What are you gabbing about?" she asked.

"Nothing," Randy said.

"Tits," I said.

"I don't even want to know, now," Susan said as she eyed my deadpan face and Randy's blushing cheeks.

"What did you come up with?" I asked, changing the subject.

"A few accounts of drunk driving and domestic altercations, and a long list of things for Charlotte Tell, a real hell-raiser, but nothing more than that," she answered.

Oh, goody, I thought to myself. We could wrap this place up in another day or two and be on our way. The thought of not coming back made me want to jump up and down. I even mapped out our return trip. We'd stick to the interstate and bypass Marion all together.

Randy drove us to a place called the Marion Grille on Maine Street. This town had a fixation for silent letters, I presumed. Trying to conjure up the sights of a long time ago, I couldn't place most of the town. It was as if it had been sucked out of my memory along with the cobwebs of nasty thoughts by a vacuum cleaner. Marion, as my mind saw fit to do, had been swept into oblivion.

The restaurant was not crowded although it was suppertime. We found a booth and seated ourselves on the green vinyl. I sat on the inside with Susan next to me, and Randy sat opposite us. The menus were on the table, and the specials were written in chalk above the cash register. There was a homespun air to the place, although it wasn't clean, but the food smelled edible. A waitress appeared at our table bearing a tray and three glasses of water in amber-colored plastic tumblers. From under the brim of my hat, I peered at her hands—beefy hands, I thought. She sweetly asked us what we wanted, and Randy began his order. He finished and Susan gave her order next. I glanced across Susan to the busily writing waitress and noticed her flat, wide face with the prominent nose. It was more like a snout, I thought, two holes visible from the front. From behind my glasses, I squinted. She had a tangle of oily, mousy hair frosted with blonde and pulled back into a short tail.

"And you?" she asked sweetly.

"A cheeseburger, fries, and a Coke, please," I asked in a subtle southern drawl that drew only the attention of my friends.

"We don't have Coke. We have Pepsi or RC," she said.

"Tea would be fine," I responded.

She wrote on her pad with her beefy hands and turned away. Her whole body was rather beefy, I thought, to match her hands. She had ample thighs and thick ankles.

"Why can't you drink Pepsi?" Susan asked.

"Because I don't like it," I said in my fake accent.

"And why are you talking like that?"

"Because, you have just met *Pig-Face*," I whispered. "And I really don't want to be recognized by her."

Although I doubted she would even know who I was, I wasn't ready to take chances. She brought our food and briefly gabbed with Randy before leaving our table for another table of customers, obviously better known to her. She sat with them and chatted endlessly, her voice ringing through the restaurant and rising in shrill laughter on occasion. We ate in near silence until Randy leaned over the table and whispered, "Well, she *does* resemble a pig." I closed my eyes and tried to squeeze back the laughter that was building in my throat. Although Sue laughed out loud, not a sound fell from these lips. I concentrated on ridding my plate of a tasteless burger and greasy fries.

"Do y'all want some dessert?" *Pig-Face* asked.

Randy scanned the menu as Sue and I shook our heads.

"I don't think so, thank-you," he answered as he accepted the ticket for dinner.

When she left the table, Susan suggested we wait for Randy in the van. He nodded in approval, and we headed out of the Marion Grille on Maine Street to the safe haven of the van. We watched as Randy paid at the register and turned to leave. He made it all the way to the van before he burst out laughing.

"Just what is so funny?" I asked.

"You have a knack of attracting all the people you want to avoid. I never saw anything like it."

"Thanks, Friend, I needed to hear that. Good thing Carlo and Jack are dead, or they would be here, too," I said.

I unfolded a map and guided Randy to the first address on the list. It was Laura's house. On the way there, I couldn't help but wonder why she was a waitress in a greasy grill with a silent vowel. Certainly, Carlo would have cared for his beloved wife. We turned onto the road to Laura's house, and I was truly surprised. It was on a road that separated the good side from the bad side—the rich from the poor. I learned a long time ago that there was no middle ground in Marion. Either a family was filthy rich or dirt poor. Both unclean, but with a big difference in the way dirt was carried.

Laura's house was a tiny wooden home with a small porch. It could have easily passed for a service quarters on the back forty of a larger home in a past century. There was a gleaming silver Lincoln Continental parked out front, and a ragamuffin lanky blond-haired man sitting on the porch drinking a beer. The rural mailbox had the name "Tell" printed on it in large white letters.

"Should I stop?" Randy asked.

"No. There really isn't a need to stop," I said.

"On to address number two?" he asked.

"Why not. I'm beginning to think there really is a God, you know," I said with the personal satisfaction that *Pig-Face* finally got what she had coming to her.

Address number two turned out to be Charlotte's house. The beloved daughter of Laura and Carlo lived in a home that was shabbier than Laura's home was. As we approached, a faded orange car pulled up, and a girl I presumed to be Charlotte came out of her house. She favored her mother with mousy hair, a chunky body with thick ankles and the ever-prominent snout for a nose. She was carrying a small child with olive skin and beautiful black curls. At first, I thought she must have been babysitting for the child's parents. There was no mention of a beloved grandchild in Carlo's obituary. But Mary's children weren't mentioned either. It could be explained by a hometown newspaper that chose only to recognize the survivors in town. Then a man emerged from the old car. He was a tall, thin, handsome African-American. Only Carlo, and possibly *Pig-Face*, would deny their child because she had a child of color, especially since it would have affected his Chamber of Commerce standing in Marion. No wonder he left town; his lily-white "friends" in high places ran him out.. Although I thought it was rather funny that this could happen to Carlo, I felt sorry for Charlotte. She couldn't help being born to the people she was born to, and she was left on her own to fend for herself. Only the strong survive in this world, I told myself. And if she has a will to live, she will, in spite of what her mother, or anybody else, has to say about it. Just like I did. I made a name for myself not because I had any backing from Carlo, but in spite of him. I found myself getting angry with him for being dead. I couldn't go to him and tell him what a rotten fuck-up he really was and how many lives he pissed away for his own gain.

"Randy, let's go check out Christine Malone's house," I said, rattled off the address, and gave him instructions on how to get there. Strangely, it was on the same road as Charlotte's house, but further up the road. As we rode, the dusty road turned into a widened paved street lined with stately pines and azalea bushes. The homes had wide driveways and well-manicured lawns.

Christine's address was marked by twin brick arcs curving toward the inner yard. A large spiked wrought iron gate that linked the two arcs was open, giving full view of a large arbor over the drive. Wisteria snaked across the arbor like a rainbow of fragrant lavender. Well back onto the property was a stately two-storied house with four large columns spaced evenly in front of a sprawling veranda.

"Holy shit!" said Randy. "Do you want me to pull into that driveway? Are we worthy?"

Susan's mouth was hanging open and I blinked twice and took off my glasses and cap trying to see better.

"No, don't pull in," I said. "Drop me off here and I will walk up and talk to her."

"What are you going to say, Sandy?" Susan asked.

"I have no fucking idea," I replied. I grabbed my notepad and laptop and stepped out at the foot of the entrance.

The walk took at least five minutes at my slow pace, and the house kept getting larger as I drew closer. I felt like Dorothy approaching the Wizard in the Emerald City. At the steps up to the veranda, I paused and took a deep breath, inhaling the sweet smell of wisteria. Slowly, I took each of the five steps and found myself at the double doors of the entrance. I rang the bell and expected a servant to answer and shoo me away for not being properly attired.

"May I help you?" a proper woman in her late thirties with perfectly layered blonde tresses asked from behind the screen.

"I don't know," I stammered. "I'm looking for Christine Malone."

"I'm Christine," she said as she opened the screen. She tilted her head to one side and her crystal eyes sparkled in recognition.

"I know you," she said. "You're Sandra Darnell, aren't you? I've read all your books. I am a big fan."

Well, that blew my cover. Of all the authors in the world, she had to read me. Now, how was I supposed to get my information? Awkwardness overcame me, and I had trouble searching for a response. It was always the same—I never could adapt to recognition, which is why I seldom left *The Hole* or South Florida.

"Thank you," I said shyly, obviously shaking.

"Come in, Ms. Darnell," Christine said as she opened the screen door.

I stepped into the massive foyer and said, "Please, call me Sandy."

"What brings you to these parts?" she asked as she led me to a sunroom off the main living room. "From what I've read about you, you call Florida home."

"That's right, I do. But, ah, well, to be honest with you, my friends and I were taking a trip through Georgia and found a house for sale in Mill Cove. We asked about it, they are considering buying it, and found that you are the owner. Call it writer's intuition, I don't know, but I get the feeling there is a story behind that house. So here I am," I said as I hoped she didn't know who my biological father was.

"Are you staying in town?" she asked.

"No. The Myrtle Beach Resort. We just drove up for the day."

"Where are your friends?"

"In a van across the street." I suddenly felt like I was a little kid answering the prodding questions of an adult. From out of nowhere, a perfectly tailored black maid appeared, and Christine told her to have someone get my friends. Then she offered an evening snack of tea and finger sandwiches. I could tell she was used to entertaining. This was more what I envisioned Carlo's style to be, and I tried to piece it together. Certainly, this woman was too savvy to fall for his bullshit.

"I see you have your notebook and computer with you. So you must be doing some writing. Well, I will try to help you as much as I can, Sandy," she said. As she spoke, I thought I caught a glimpse of sadness behind those shimmering eyes. I heard the door open and was pleased to see Randy and Susan enter the room. They looked more at ease than I did as they seated themselves on a couch opposite me.

"These are my friends, Randy and Susan Clark," I said. "They were interested in the house in Mill Cove."

Randy and Susan picked up on the line, and offered very little information from then on.

Christine sat back in her chair as if she were a judge tallying a rap sheet to pronounce sentence on three criminals. She was cool, collected, and totally in control of the situation.

"You wouldn't like that house," she said. "Or Mill Cove. It is an awful place. Nothing but rednecks there."

As she spoke in her perfect diction with a hint of an accent, I became convinced that she was not a native of Marion. This strange woman cast such a spell over me that I couldn't even think straight. It was Randy who saved my cover.

"Why? What is it about Mill Cove that is so bad? We found the house to be everything we could want," he said with conviction.

"No. It's not for you," she answered. "Better to let a local person have the house. I don't want it. In fact, I'd like to get rid of this monstrosity, too, and move back home, but I have business here."

Christine was holding something back, and I gathered all my strength to pry it out of her.

"I know about demons, Christine. They have chased me all my life. Some are still haunting me. That's where I get a lot of my stories from; I change the names of the demons and pour out my soul. Perhaps you need to rid yourself of whatever it is that is haunting you, but to assume that the haunts will follow someone else is preposterous. Look at Randy and Susan. They are happy and very much in love. I believe they would fit nicely in the house in Mill Cove," I said as if giving a speech before the United Nations General Assembly.

Susan and Randy looked at me with awe. The words passed my lips so effortlessly and convincingly. Damn, I'm good, I told myself.

"But these are not ordinary demons," Christine said, her eyes misting slightly.

"I wish I could tell you the story, but it is too painful to even think about. Just trust me. You don't want that house. Would it help convince you if I told you there was a murder there?"

Susan, Randy and I shared a look of shock at her statement.

"Murder?" I gasped.

"Yes. It was not proven, you know, at least not by the local police. But I know it was murder and I know who did it. You see, it was someone here in Marion,, and I have to stay here to make that person pay. I am not a vindictive person, but the act was so very cruel that I have no choice," Christine said.

From the grand foyer, the sound of the front door shook Christine from her words. Footsteps neared the sunroom as the last hint of daylight gave way. We turned and gazed as a well-dressed man of subtle distinction entered the room and exchanged a loving glance with Christine. He looked at Randy, Susan and me and said, "Hello."

"Allow me to introduce you to my husband, Brad Malone," Christine said as she introduced Randy and Susan and then me.

"Christine has a library of your books," the handsome Brad said.

"Must be a small collection," I said lightly.

"She takes her reading seriously. What brings you here to Marion?" he asked.

"A most unusual twist of circumstances, Dear. I can't wait to tell you the whole story," Christine said in a most peculiar manner.

"Well, it has been nice meeting you, and I do hope you will autograph your books for my Christine. Now, I must excuse myself. I have business to attend to," Brad said before he turned and left the room.

Christine turned her head and stared out at the darkening garden until Brad was well out of hearing range.

"Can I meet you somewhere tomorrow?" she asked, "I can come to the beach and we can meet for lunch at the Resort. For some reason, as strange as it sounds, I feel the need to tell you about the house, but I can't now. I suppose you have all kinds of people that tell you stories, don't you? But this one is different. Please meet me for lunch."

I didn't have the heart to tell her that nobody to my knowledge has ever stopped me to tell me any strange stories—except Pudge. But few of his stories made it to print in my books. Still, there was a sound of near desperation in her voice, and I believed she really just wanted to talk to someone.

"Whatever time you get there is fine with me. I have no plans for tomorrow," I said, even though I was planning to leave the state. What the hell, I told myself, one more day couldn't hurt.

"Thank you," she whispered, "thank you all."

She showed us to her library where she did have my books prominently displayed on the shelf. I placed my signature on the inside cover of each one with the inscription: "Dear Christine, Thank you for your warm hospitality. You made my trip through Marion a most memorable experience. Your friend, Sandra Darnell." Then I carefully dated each one and handed them back to her for their replacement among her collection. We followed her to the door and said a subdued good night. She squeezed my hand,

and as our eyes met, I definitely found the pain burning behind them. This woman had a very tragic story to tell, and I could hardly wait to hear it.

Randy led the way to the van, and we eased out of Christine's driveway slowly and without speaking. He drove back toward the highway and was at least five miles out of Marion before he opened his mouth to speak.

"What the fuck is going on?" he asked.

"I wish I knew," I said as I cringed at the recollection of Christine's words about someone in Marion murdering Carlo.

"The only pieces I can put together are that Christine knew Carlo, although she never mentioned his name. And Christine either knows who killed Carlo or she thinks she does."

"I bet she thinks Laura did it," Susan offered.

"I don't know who she thinks did what, but I have a funny suspicion I will find out tomorrow," I said.

I turned my thoughts to Pudge. If the person who killed Carlo had no link to Pudge, then the person who killed Pudge could have been our first suspect—Steve the Slime. That would explain the missing box. Oh shit, I thought as I leaned my head against the window, I'm back at the beginning, and I don't think I'll ever find out what happened to my friend. I squeezed my eyes closed in an attempt to clear the tangled fray of information I had and tried to convince myself to just head back to Florida without completing the planned trip. I fell asleep and had *The Dream* again before we were halfway to Myrtle Beach.

It was a good thing I managed to get some rest, dream or no dream, as I knew getting real sleep after meeting Christine would be impossible. The closest I would come to sleep after arriving at our room was a double rum and half a pack of cigarettes.

I called Shane and explained how to download the information I was sending via computer. He listened well and read back the information.

"Mom, what's up? There's something strange in your voice," my son queried.

"Nothing, Shane. Really. I'm just tired," I said with as much conviction as I could muster.

"You have that weird dream again?" he asked.

"Every now and then. Nothing to worry about," I said and found myself getting tired of hearing everybody talk about my fucking dreams. I wondered how he found out about it and then came to the conclusion Randy or Susan told him.

"I mentioned that dream to Mara. She said it was sexual," Shane said.

"Shane, don't go telling people about my fucking dreams."

"I was just trying to help."

"It isn't sexual, Shane. It's about something else."

"How do you know?"

"How does Mara know?" I countered.

"Look, let's just drop it," my son said, much to my satisfaction.

We closed the conversation on a higher note, but I could not erase the resentment in my voice. How could my son go around telling strangers the privacy of my dreams?

"What's wrong?" Susan asked as she came into my room.

"Nothing. Except Shane told Mara about my dream, and she told him *The Dream* is sexual," I said. I looked her squarely in her eyes and said, "I know you told him about *The Dream*."

She suppressed a slight smile and answered, "Yes. I told him. But I told him not to tell anyone. He must be bothered by it though, or he wouldn't have told Mara. Sexual, huh?"

"Oh, fuck you," I said.

"I don't have the problem," she answered smugly and sat down on the bed.

"Susan, for Chrissake, it's not a problem. It's a dream. A stupid, fucking irritating dream. And it is not sexual. I don't have any sexual problems, other than the lack of a mate, which I'm not sure I want anyway," I spat at her.

My mind was garbled with rum, Pudge, Carlo, Christine, and the whole atmosphere of this trip into my personal hell of bad dreams. No wonder I was having nightmares. I missed my home, Amaretto, and my work. I missed watching the spring turn into summer - the cool nights melding into sticky, soft tropical nights. I missed hearing the doves in the surrounding groves. I missed sitting on the porch watching Mickey Dog chase lizards around the yard. I missed my own life, space, and thoughts. I hated this trip. Hated the people I was digging up, and hated not having the answers to questions that were just beginning to come to my mind. I hated the fucking hovering man that was with *The Moon Lady*. The hotels, the van, and even Randy and Susan were getting to me, grinding my nerves to frayed edges that were popping and snapping like breakfast cereal in milk. And to have Susan tell Shane about *The Dream*, and have him pass it on to a woman I didn't even know, really grated on me.

"Just go away. I want to be alone," I said.

She left and I turned out the lights and opened the drapes and the door to the balcony. I sank into a lounge chair on the balcony, propped my feet on the railing, and watched the stars play on the swells off the shore. Forcing the thoughts out of my mind, I let my body wander somewhere beyond the horizon to a quiet place where no land was in sight. With the open sea all around me, soothing my mind and drowning the thoughts, I let the tide sweep me away.

Morning came too quickly to my disturbed sleep. It was more peaceful on the balcony, but still uncomfortable. I resolved that I had grown accustomed to having little sleep. I showered and dragged out the best clothes I had with me, a simple suit, and waited for the phone to ring. Randy and Susan were in the living room eating breakfast when I emerged from my room.

"Feeling better?" Sue asked.

"A little. Any calls?"

"Nope. Not yet."

As soon as I sat down, the phone rang. Christine was waiting in the restaurant downstairs. I took a notepad with me, no laptop this time, and tried to look as calm as possible as I entered the restaurant and made my way to her table. She had chosen a table in the back secluded from the other patrons by a wall of fake palms. As I approached the table, she smiled from under a wide-brimmed hat.

"You look more like I envisioned you," said Christine. "The suit fits you much better than the ragged jeans you had on yesterday."

"Well, I don't make it a habit to be a fashion plate. And if you think I sit around all day and write in a suit or a flowery summer dress, you are sadly misinformed," I said as I motioned the waiter to the table.

I needed rum. Quick. I could not figure out what the ex-urbanite woman wanted to tell me, and I was tired of playing games and coming up empty.

"So, what is it you want to tell me?" I asked bluntly.

"I don't know if I want to tell you anything other than your friends shouldn't buy the house in Mill Cove," Christine said.

My patience was wearing thin. When it gets this thin, I am likely to lash out at the nearest person, whether deserving or not, and Christine had no idea how close she was to getting blasted away from the table and back to her little southern mansion.

I sighed. "Christine, I'm sorry if I sound terse, but I have little time and there are things I need to know. If I can't find the answers here, I have to move on. I am on a tight schedule and my time is very precious."

The waiter returned with my rum and brought Christine a glass of white wine. She sipped from it twice and her eyes met mine.

"Okay. The game's over. This is what I have to tell you about the house. I was in love with a man, and we bought the house in Mill Cove together. The reason I live in Marion is Brad is an executive with a company that moved there from Cincinnati. I met this other man, Carlo, at a social function. He was there with his wife. We met, fell in love, and decided to leave Marion together. We spent a weekend at the country club in Mill Cove and decided it would be a pleasant place to settle down.

"But his wife is this snooty little whore; excuse me, that rules the roost in Marion. She was born and raised there and had nothing until Carlo married her. He loved me and was ready to leave her and she knew it. She tried to get what she could of his money, but his money was mine. She even tried to have an affair with Brad to get back at me. But I don't love Brad and he doesn't love me. We use each other for social purposes and pretty much live our own lives. Brad has another love interest and I know it. But Carlo's wife made a big deal out of trying to bed Brad."

This was a typical Carlo story and I tried not to look bored. I didn't have the heart to tell her that Carlo was having an affair with Vera in Mill Cove or that he fucked everything that walked past him. Most of all, I tried not to look bored. I ordered another rum.

"Do you always drink rum like that?" she asked.

"Yes. Go on."

"Anyway," she continued, "she tried to start all these cat fights with me on every occasion. She said she'd kill me before I took her Carlo away. What she didn't know is that I am a lawyer, and Brad's money is Brad's, but mine is mine. And her threats were starting to mount. Carlo signed all his belongings over to me before we left for Mill Cove, so he was penniless except for his car.

"We left Marion together and set up house in Mill Cove. We were going to file for divorces in Marion and thought it would be better if we didn't go back into town together, so I went back to Marion and he stayed behind."

Fucking Vera, I said to myself.

"Christine," I said, "I think I know where this is heading."

"Please," she said, her eyes getting teary, "let me finish. I need to do this."

I nodded and finished the rum.

"When I returned to Marion, I went to my attorney's office and filed for divorce. When I left the building, Laura, that's her name, was waiting. She made a big scene in the middle of Maine Street. She threatened me again, but this time she said, 'You will never have Carl; I'll kill him first.' Being a refined person, I just walked away with her shouting threats after me. I went to Brad's house and told him what I had decided, and we agreed to part amicably. I retired to my room and called Carlo. He said he was busy planting a garden at our new house, and I told him about Laura. He laughed it off.

"I left the next day. When I got to Mill Cove, I felt strange. I can't explain it. But there was Carlo, working on the garden. We went inside and he told me he planned on going back to Marion the following day. We sat and talked for a couple of hours, and he went out to pick up his gardening tools while I went in to take a shower. As I got out of the shower, I heard sirens coming closer, and I looked out the front window. There was Carlo, on the ground, with a few neighbors standing around.

"I dashed out the door and ran to him. It was too late. He was dead."

Christine's eyes were damp, and her hands were shaking as she drank her wine.

"Don't you see?" she pleaded, "it was Laura who killed him. So I came back to Marion and reconciled with Brad. But I have everything Carlo owned. And my vow is to make her pay. Already, she has had to go to work as a waitress."

Some things never ceased to amaze me. Matters of the heart were the most confusing. For some reason, I could never see the sense in playing little love games, especially if they were destructive. And I had no patience for cat fights. Randy was right. I wasn't a real woman. How could I be? Here was a bright, well-educated, beautiful woman who fell for Carlo and made a vow to cause destruction to his pig-faced widow for killing him. Even though, if she thought about it long enough, there were doubts that Laura did kill Carlo.

"And seeing her that way makes you feel good?" I asked, trying to find some insight on how I should act if I were to awaken tomorrow as a real woman.

"No," she sobbed. "But there is some satisfaction there. I know I could never get her convicted. Especially not in Marion."

I don't know, Christine. He could have been killed by accident," I said, sounding as hollow as the police did when they told me Pudge had committed suicide.

"No, he was killed deliberately. I know it. And that is what I am dealing with. That story told, you can see why I don't want your friends to buy the house, can't you? I mean, I do have some respect for you," she said.

"Yes, I can. I will talk them out of it," I said as I looked at my watch. "Now, I really have to be going. Thank you for sharing that with me."

"It was a pleasure meeting you. I will continue to buy your books, you know. I can only hope that this story doesn't wind up in a novel," Christine said, almost pleading.

"Don't worry. I have no desire to write a book about love—good or bad—I stick to my stories of the sea and the tropics," I said, standing to leave.

We shook hands, and she pulled me close and kissed my cheek. God, I dislike touchy-feely people. But I let it slide this time and said my farewell to Christine Malone, a scorned woman on a mission of destruction. I couldn't tell her that I doubted Laura had what it took to kill someone. She was a mouthy bitch who said stupid things, but had no clue as to what real life was about. Not until now anyway, when she had to actually work for a living.

Chalk it up to another major fuck-up on Carlo's part. As I entered the elevator, I looked up and mouthed a thank-you to God for taking Carlo off this earth. When I returned to the room, I relayed the whole Christine story to Randy and Susan and told them why I didn't buy it. Susan said Christine's story at least made sense. There was a definite motive there, while my theory that Carlo, Jack, and Pudge, and maybe Steve, were tied together, was grabbing at a phantom thought. Susan made sense, but I was determined to hedge on.

We decided that we had enough of this place and would leave the next morning. As we headed for our rooms, I turned and smiled at Randy.

"What is it?" he asked. "You have that grin on your face."

"If Christine tells that story to every potential buyer, she'll never sell that house," I said.

Randy shook his head, smiled, and disappeared into the bedroom. In a few minutes, I heard Susan laugh.

"Only you could think of that!" she yelled from their room.

Chapter 6

If quarters were guns

I don't think I was ever so happy to leave a place in my entire life, with the exception of the night a few acquaintances and I were asked to leave Cozumel because we were obviously drunk and disorderly. We figured we had to have been pretty bad to get kicked out of another country, although none of us could quite remember the reason. As for me, I could barely remember being there and every time I have been back since that episode, it has been under a different name. Let's just say we may have been drunk, but not stupid. We were presented with a choice: jail or expulsion. We choose the latter. The circumstances may have been different, and the weather, but this was positively the worst experience ever. Nobody likes to come face to face with their past, especially when there is so much pain and deceit left behind. And, although I have developed a high threshold of both physical and mental discomfort, some mental anguish is nearly impossible to suppress without ill side effects. This was one trip that guaranteed a lasting scar. The wounds had festered and oozed long enough, and were now healed, but the red, raised scar formed over the opening would never heal.

THE AMARETTO

Somewhere near Virginia, Randy mentioned to me that it was my fault for not forgetting the whole thing years ago. I told him I had forgotten most of it, but some pain remained. He said he had never met anyone who took things so personally and I should just forget the whole experience past and present. The death of Carlo, Laura's penance as a waitress—with a guardian angel named Christine making sure she stayed humble—coupled with the realization that Carlo's daughter, Charlotte, was the one who toppled the great aspiring Carlo, gave me an eerie joy. I had nothing to feel responsible for. He did himself in, just like my mother told me he would. And as I thought about what my mother would say when I told her all the details, Alex crept into my mind. A wave of sorrow and guilt rushed over me. I wondered how he would have reacted to my trip and the fact that I went digging up shit that should have been buried a long time ago. In one way, he would have been mildly disappointed. But in a bigger way, he would have applauded my actions. Call it fatherly pride, but Alex never condemned anything I did or said. I was his princess and I wallowed in it. Even when my mother would utter her favorite line to me, "Sandra! Watch your language!" he would say, "At least she calls 'em the way they are." What a man. Sometimes the logic of my mind runs a straight track.

The next step in my thinking was that the reason I was sans mate was because I was looking for another Alex, and he didn't exist. Sure, Lee came close, but not all the way. And I never compromised. So the wait continued. Until that very day, I would be alone and I would enjoy it. There really was no reason to go "find somebody" as my sister would tell me I needed to do. I was happiest when I was alone. No person in their right mind would put up with my moodiness, drinking, and spur-of-the-moment excursions to the ocean. Fuck the world, I concluded; I was true to my own self and an island that no person could approach. And that was the way it was meant to be, so I accepted it and vowed to continue making the most of it.

As we headed even further north, topping Delaware and moving dangerously close to New Jersey and the biggest skeleton I could dig up, I took the wheel for the first time. Susan and Randy left me alone for the better part of the trip from South Carolina and concentrated on the driving while I wrote in the back of the van. Surprisingly, I got a lot done. When we made it to Atlantic City, I made a vow to call Paul Barclay's office in New York and send him a summary and my notes on the next book. This trip played an integral part of the unfolding plot, but I didn't have an ending yet. Paul, knowing me perhaps as well as Randy, would have to trust me.

Nearing Atlantic City, I recalled how I left New Jersey before the casinos opened and had never returned to that area. We decided it would be of interest to find a hotel on the boardwalk and get some serious gambling done before heading up to Berkeley. The weather had turned blustery at best when we arrived. Gray clouds shrouded the ocean in a veil of obscurity. The cold, stinging mist chilled my depths. I craved hot coffee to ward off the cold and was pissed that all I had as a cover was a jean jacket. For some reason, and it happens all the time, I had forgotten that March is not the signal for warm weather all over the country. And although April was but one week away, the Atlantic City temperature was barely fifty degrees.

"So this is what Atlantic City is like," Susan said as she stood on the balcony and looked out over the boardwalk.

"Actually, no, this isn't what it is like, Sue. The real Atlantic City is on the other side of the hotel, but I wouldn't advise going over there if you value your life," I said. "At least that's what I've heard."

"Well, do you recommend we enjoy this part of it or wallow in other people's sorrow?" Randy asked smugly.

"I think I have enough to wallow in already. There is enough depressing shit in my own life without having to see someone else's misfortune," Susan answered.

"I suggest we stretch out, relax, and have something to eat before the night finally falls, and we can take a walk on the famous boardwalk," Randy said.

"In all my years, I never thought I'd wind up in New Jersey on a vacation. This is one for the record books."

He turned and looked at his wife.

"Gee, Randy," Sue said, "I really appreciate the way you take me to all the finer places in life."

I settled onto my bed and laughed behind a raised room service menu.

"Hey, partner," Randy said.

"You talking to me?" I asked and peered over the top of the menu.

"Here's a good luck charm," he said as he tossed a roll of quarters at me.

Ahhh, my reflexes were not dulled by rum, I thought, as I reached up with one hand and caught the missile.

"Hey, thanks. I will put this to good use tonight," I said as I slipped the roll into the inner pocket of my jacket.

We ordered some food, ate, and took a nap until night fell. Susan wanted to see the lights of the boardwalk under cloak of darkness, and we obliged her. She was trying to conceal her excitement, but Randy and I knew she had never seen anything like this before, and we indulged her childlike wonder at the people parading the boardwalk. The cold rain didn't faze her or Randy; I didn't want to be the one to bitch about the weather, so I concealed my shivering as best I could. We stopped at a small shop on the boardwalk, so I could replenish my supply of cigarettes, and as we stepped back out to the cold night, I caught a glimpse of something familiar—*The Floater*. Nudging Susan sharply in the ribs, I nodded in his direction.

"Holy shit," she said, "What the hell is *he* doing here?"

"Tell me I'm not merely paranoid. Tell me that we aren't being followed on this trip. Tell me something other than all the shit you've been telling me," I said to both her and Randy. "Something strange is happening here and I want to fucking know what it is!"

"Calm down for chrissake," Randy said as my eyes followed *The Floater* down the boardwalk. "Jesus! You've got that evil look in your eyes; Sandy and I don't like it. Don't do anything stupid. If he is following us, he's harmless alone. We don't know if there is anyone else with him. Just calm down and play it cool."

He had a hold on my arm as the man floated out of sight. At that moment, the boardwalk became a throng of people as one of the shows let out, and the audience packed us against the outer glass of the store. The cold air was nothing compared to the chill that emanated from within, and I realized I was not going to be able to contain myself much longer. As Randy released his grip on my arm, I caught a glimpse of *The Floater* walking north on the outer edge of the crowd. As the familiar bravery mode set in, I broke free and shoved and pushed my way across the sea of people. I fell in about fifteen people behind my target and set my eyes on his back. This time, I was determined to get answers. He picked up his pace, and I kept up with him. He turned, caught my eyes with those hypnotic ice blues, and quickened his pace even more. I was almost running to keep up and found myself gaining. The other people on the boardwalk melted from view, and I shoved the stragglers in my way aside. I heard Randy and Susan calling me, but I heeded nothing. *The Floater* began running, and I, reaching deep inside and summoning my reserve energy, burst ahead in the chase. He exited the boardwalk and made his way to the water's edge. I jumped over the wooden barrier and toppled to the sand, not taking my eyes off him. I was making time in the sand, despite the pounding of my heart and the dry coldness in my throat that was beginning to ache. Too much rum and cigarettes and too little exercise had taken its toll on my body. He was within five feet when I summoned all my remaining power and lunged through the air and wrapped my arms around his waist forcing him to the sand. He was in a half-turn when he fell, and with the weight of my body, I held him down with my left arm pushing hard against his throat. I felt a heavy weight in my side drop onto his abdomen and remembered the roll of quarters. My right hand thrust in my pocket arranging the concealed roll to a point and jutting him with it.

"Don't shoot!" he said, and I knew my bluff worked.

"I won't, if you don't scream," I said coldly.

"I won't."

"Who the fuck are you, and why are you following me?" I demanded.

He opened his eyes widely and locked his eyes onto mine.

"I'm not following you. I have no idea what you are talking about, lady."

"Look, I saw you at the bar on No Name Key, and I saw you in Myrtle Beach, and now you're here. Coincidence? I don't think so. Now talk," I rasped as I poked him harder with the roll of coins.

"My name is Bill. And I live on Big Pine Key. I saw you and your friends at the No Name, and I heard what you and *The Moon*

Lady said to each other. I fish for a living, and I thought it would be an adventure to follow you. That's all. There is nobody else with me. I am alone. I don't know what you are doing, or anything, and I won't tell anybody about your trip. I don't know anything else," he said in a shaky voice.

"What the fuck are you doing, Sandy?" Randy's out-of-breath voice rang out from overhead.

"Trying to get some answers. What does it look like I'm doing?" I spat.

"Please!" Bill said, looking up at Randy, "tell her not to shoot me."

"Don't shoot him, Sandy!" Randy said.

"I won't, as long as he keeps talking!" I screamed.

"I swear I have nothing else to say!" he pleaded.

"There is nothing more repulsive than a sniveling man-boy," I said looking deep into his familiar eyes and pressing my arm tighter against his neck. "I have something to say, and you better listen real good, Bill. Go back to Big Pine. Leave me the fuck alone. I am not above hurting you if you get too close. Do you understand me?"

"Yes!"

"Now get out of my sight, and don't ever let me see you again."

As I loosened my arm from his neck and eased the roll of quarters from his side, I heard voices from behind Randy. The cops. Oh shit, just what I needed.

"What's going on here?" a fat, balding officer with a limp asked. "Nothing, officer," Bill answered to my surprise. "We were just playing a game of chase, and she got me."

We stood up and faced the cop. He eyed us and let his gaze stray down to the pocket of my jacket where my hand held the quarters.

"What have you got there?" he asked.

I pulled my hand and the roll from my pocket.

"Quarters," I said innocently. "For the slots."

"Well, good luck," he nodded. "Enjoy your stay here, but keep your game playing to a minimum. These old people don't like getting shoved around the boardwalk." He turned and walked away shaking his head and muttering something about tourists. I looked at Bill who was standing beside me.

"Quarters?" he asked as a slight blush washed over his face.

"I hate guns," I said. "It got the job done anyway. But, don't you underestimate me, Kid. I'll kill you if I see you again."

Randy looked at Bill and said, "She's capable, Kid. Trust me. Now make sure you get your ass away from us. Hear?"

"Yes, sir. I'll pack tonight. I promise," he said as he turned and walked back toward the small crowd that had gathered on the boardwalk.

"You asshole," Randy said. "You could have gotten killed, or wound up in jail, or scared him to death. What the fuck is wrong with you?"

"I have no idea, but *The Floater* ain't going to be bothering us again. Let's go find Sue," I said as we made our way back.

"Quarters," Randy muttered and smiled. "You scared the shit out of someone with a roll of fucking quarters. You are amazing."

"I know. And this roll of quarters is going to win us some money. I can feel it," I replied.

And I was right. By the time we left Atlantic City, we had an extra thousand dollars in our pockets and nobody following us compliments of Randy and his toss of a benign roll of quarters.

Chapter 7

Glad to See You. Now, I'm Leaving

We made our way to Watchung, some fifteen miles from Berkeley, where we rented two motel rooms adjoined by a door. We figured we could ensure our privacy in the event we got pissed at each other and maintain our closeness when we weren't pissed. The first thing I did was call Paul and apologize for not getting in touch with him sooner. I told him that I would be in New York within the next two days, and I would go over the details of the book. He said that from what I told him about the trip and the three deaths, it would make for a great story. He was eager to hear what the ending would be. I don't think he was nearly as eager to find that out as I was. My only consolation was that *The Floater*, Bill, wasn't on our tail anymore. It was one thing investigating the murders of the people you loved and hated, it was quite another doing it under the watchful eye of a snooping fisherman from the Keys.

The second thing I did was call Shane who apologized for telling my dream to Mara. He didn't apologize for telling me that the whole dream was sexual, but he did at least say he was sorry for invading my much-coveted privacy. So far, he said, *The Hole* was still in one piece, and Mickey Dog was healthy. And, perhaps most important of all, there were no dust balls at my mother's house. He said she had called and told him she would be returning next week. I promised I would be home by then. I was extremely travel weary and doubted we would spend much time in New Jersey. Shane also said he met a "real nice woman." Trying to sound happy, I recalled that was the very same thing he told me when he met the last bimbo. I uploaded and sent some more computer files home, and he captured them for me before we ended our conversation.

Randy came into my room and asked if we could eat something and then take a quick drive through Berkeley so he could get a feel for the place while Susan took a rest. We stopped for burgers, and I kept a paranoid eye open, not for Bill, but for a glimpse of a familiar face from my past. I had no desire to run into anybody I may have grown up with. As far as I was concerned, there were no friendships I wanted to rekindle. Call it the Floridian's paranoia that people from up here would find out where you lived and make their way to your house every winter for eternity. I know it happens. It happened to my mother for several years before Alex died. Then she wised up and started spending her winters in other places like France.

As we drove toward Berkeley, dusk was turning the northeastern sky to dusty lavender. The chill of the oncoming night was pleasant for once. The sights and sounds conjured up happy memories of my short childhood, and we turned onto Butler Avenue where I lived as a small girl. When my family moved here from the bustle of Newark, it was like discovering the Promised Land. There were actual lawns spreading around large houses, and the night brought the silence of the suburbs so intensely that I used to hum to make sure I hadn't lost my hearing. On the crest of the Butler Avenue hill was a large gray house—my old home. There was a FOR SALE sign out front. Funny how everything we wanted to see was for sale. Ignoring the sign, I turned into the driveway and sat for a moment soaking up my past. There was the old stump I used to sit on and my mother's rose garden on the side of the house. The trees were smaller than I remembered, and although the yard was large, it didn't cover as much ground as it did when I was smaller.

"What are you doing?" Randy asked.

"I just have to see if they will let me inside. I don't know why, but I have to try," I replied.

"Well, I can't very well let you do this alone, can I?" he said.

"No. Come on," I said as I exited the van.

I slowly walked across the flagstone walk taking in each colored slate and recalling each crack as I went along. I made my way up the four slate steps and paused at the front door. I looked over my shoulder past Randy to a duplicate house across the street.

"What's over there?" he asked.

"That," I responded, "was where my father Alex lived."

I rang the bell, and a tall, robust woman with dyed black hair and a nasty habitual nervous nose twitch answered the door.

"Excuse me, ma'am, I'm sorry to bother you, but I grew up in this house, and I was wondering if you could let me in to see it." I tried not to sound like a common thief, or even worse, a nut case, but my words sounded phony even to me. She studied my face and I saw a slight trace of recognition.

"Sandra Darnell!" she said, "I know you! You mean you used to live here? It can't really be you."

"Well, it is me," I said as I fumbled in my purse for my driver's license. "Here, look."

"I'll be. By all means, come on in," she said as she flung the screen door open and welcomed Randy and me inside the house.

To my adult eyes, the house had shrunk along with the yard, but it was still a grand old house. Things were pretty much the same since I last tread these floors some twenty-two years ago. This was something I had always wanted to do, but never had the courage or time to accomplish. And how lucky I was that all the pertinent people on this trip were avid fiction readers!

"May I get you some coffee, Miss Darnell?" the woman asked.

"Yes, please. That would be nice. And please, call me Sandy—everybody calls me Sandy—and this is one of my closest friends, Randy Clark," I said as I pointed to Randy and followed her from the foyer to the kitchen. From the recreation room one floor below, I could hear the laughter of children as they watched television.

"Excuse me," I said, "I didn't get your name."

"Oh, I am sorry," the woman said as she poured a cup of coffee for me and one for Randy, "Jenny DeLizza. And you may call me Jenny."

We sat and drank coffee and made light conversation. Jenny never took her eyes off me and acted in that irritating way people do when they see someone they admire.

"So, what brings you to Berkeley?" she asked.

"I have a sister who lives not too far away, and to be honest with you, this is something I have always wanted to do, but was never able to bring myself to do it. I figured if I didn't do it this time, I may never have another chance."

"Yes. I understand the feeling," she said. Then she called for her children to be quiet even though I assured her that they weren't bothering me, which was a lie and Randy knew it. I was the picture of politeness to my fan, and he was getting a real kick out of it.

"I suppose you'd like to poke around the rest of the house?" Jenny asked.

"Yes," I responded, "I'd like that."

"Well, go right ahead."

"I'd feel better if you accompanied us. That is, if you don't mind the fact that I may reminisce out loud a time or two. You know what they say about writers—we're weird."

She laughed as she got up from her chair and led the way up the stairs and to the left toward the master bedroom. This had been my mother's room, the big room, and it really looked small to my adult eyes. Off the master bedroom was a small room that Jenny had converted to a sewing room. This was my very first solo bedroom, but it didn't last long I told her. I recalled how in the summer, the early morning light used to come through the window with a vengeance and cast the brightest light across my pillow, waking me to a new day.

We left the master suite and went to the middle bedroom—the room I shared with my sister when she was in high school. When she got married, it was my room, my very first sanctuary. But I couldn't go in because it was also a violated sanctuary, and I recalled lying on my bed when the door opened, and a drunk Jack Truitt, entrusted by my mother to babysit me, came in and crawled all over me while holding his hand tightly over my mouth. I remember the pain and shame I felt when he forced himself on me and the threats he made that kept me from telling my mother what happened. Next to that was the room that once belonged to my grandmother. And next to that was the large guest bath.

We descended the stairs to the living room, and Jenny went to the recreation room ahead of us to quiet the children before we went down. As I descended the steps, I recalled a time when we had no air conditioning and used to spend the hottest summer nights sleeping here where it was cooler. I also remembered my grandmother coming home late and going directly down the stairs to watch the news. There was a room at the foot of the stairs that was decorated to suit a guest—it once belonged to my brother who died in his teens—and a bathroom to the right of that at the end of the small hall. The large recreation room was filled with toys and four children. They sat in a row on the couch, fingers in their mouths, watching television.

"This is Miss Darnell," Jenny said to the children, "she has traveled a long way to visit this house. She used to live here."

The children looked at me quizzically the way children do whenever any grownup says that another grownup was once a child—they just can't believe it. I smiled and made light conversation with the children. They were all too adorable with their big brown eyes and dark brown hair. They all looked very much like Jenny, except they didn't twitch their faces. In a short time, Jenny led us to the basement, which had been transformed into a barroom with a partition concealing the washer and dryer. The room had stained-glass lamps and a large pool table in the middle. This was the type of room I would have liked to have in my house, I thought, then discarded the idea because I was not into entertaining, and this was definitely an entertaining room. There was a very old mint-condition Wurlitzer Juke Box against the far wall. Jenny said it was a gift from her father.

We ascended the stairs from the basement—the room I used to retreat to when I had to ponder scary stories of ghosts and Godzilla—and went to the back porch. It hadn't changed, except it was much smaller than I remembered, like the rest of the house. We exited the porch to the back yard and the flagstone patio that ran the length of the house. The old oak tree that my mother used to stand under hanging out laundry was bigger than I recalled. It was still there after countless lightning strikes during summer storms. I could hear the voices of neighborhood children engrossed in games of hopscotch and hide-and-seek, and I realized that some things would never change. Childhood would still sound the same in a hundred years, and this old neighborhood had heard more than its share. But it remained pleasant enough. We went back into the house and made our way to the kitchen for another cup of coffee.

"You will autograph your books for me, won't you?" Jenny asked.

"Of course. It's the least I could do after I barged into your home without warning, and you were kind enough to show me around," I replied.

She disappeared up the stairs, and I looked at Randy.

"Funny," I said, "some things change, and some things stay the same. The sights and sounds outside are as if nothing has changed and no time has passed. I half-expected to hear the kid next door plinking on the piano."

He smiled. "You have a lot more courage than me. I don't ever want to go back to where I lived when I was younger. Too many bad vibes there I can live without."

Jenny returned with the books, and I autographed them. She saw us to the door, and before I left, I asked her why she was selling the house.

"Because," she said, her gaze dropping to the ground, "my husband left me for a little southern girl from South Carolina."

My spine froze. History repeats itself. Maybe it was the house that held a curse.

"That's too bad. I'm so sorry to hear that," I offered.

"That's okay. I don't think I would take him back if he returned, which I know he doesn't want," she said, then added, "I'm worth more than that."

Randy and I got into the van and backed out of the driveway. We waved to Jenny, and as we made our way down the hill in the streetlight-illuminated darkness, a man eased his car into the driveway of what used to be Alex's house. For a fleeting second, I swore I could see Alex getting out of his car, turning and waving toward my old house before entering his own. It was a strange sensation, both disturbing and comforting at the same time, and I found myself wishing with all my might that I could go back into the past and right all the wrongs that had been done to me, my mother, and Alex. Randy was staring at me as I drove past so many memories on the sides of each road.

"What?" I asked.

"It could have been worse," my friend said, "you could have grown up in Malibu like I did."

I grinned. He was right. There were an awful lot of strange people in Malibu.

"Where are we going now?" he asked.

"Rum," I said. "I need rum, and there has to be a bar somewhere downtown."

"Okay, I'll let you have a drink, but we should call Sue," he said.

"Deal. You call Sue, and I'll have a drink."

We pulled into the parking lot of a grocery store and shopping center. At the corner of the lot was a place called Park Place. It looked about as good a place as any for a drink, so we parked and went in. As soon as I opened the door, I could hear the music. Randy's type of music, although I have to admit, it sure sounded good. Randy loved all those oldies from the late fifties and early sixties. I felt old all of a sudden, but not crotchety old. Old like I was wiser and the music still sounded good.

"I can stand this place," Randy said as he gently steered me toward the phone.

As he called Sue, I leaned against the wall and listened to the voices when the music paused. I peered around the corner and saw a table against the back wall and motioned to Randy that I was going to claim it for us. As I strolled across the room, I felt eyes on me. I didn't belong here, and the patrons could tell there was a foreigner among them. I kept my eyes focused solely on the table and sat down with my back against the wall. I ordered rum for me and a beer for Randy and took a deep breath before letting my eyes scan the faces of the room. At least half of the faces were older versions of those I went to school with, and I smiled to myself. I gave no indication that I recognized anyone and turned my concentration to the rum in front of me. Randy sat down, and again, the heads turned. I ignored them and focused on the face of my friend.

"So, how's Susan?" I asked.

"Sleepy and wondering if we are having an affair," he answered.

"You shit. You wish."

"Try again. The last thing I want to do is have an affair with you. I wouldn't stand a chance. My ego would be shattered. I couldn't handle it," he said as he took a long sip of his beer. "No. Susan is more my type."

A chipper young woman with long, feathery blonde hair, a lot of makeup, and a tray stood beside our table and smiled.

"Can I get you something to eat? Our specials are chicken wings, nachos with cheese, fried mozzarella, and grilled chicken breast fillets," she said.

Oh, joy, I thought, same old food. I drained my glass.

"I'll have another rum and a cheeseburger. My friend will have a cheeseburger and another beer."

She wrote it all down and disappeared.

"No wings or fried cheese?" asked Randy.

"Not tonight, Kid. Although the way everybody keeps staring at us, I can say that with one more rum, I will stand up and announce that we won't be dining on fried cheese and bottled water and that it will be a cold day in hell before we dress like they do in their suits. And I might let on that we prefer to spend our spare time scraping the bottom of old shrimp boats."

"Hey, the reason they're looking this way is we have tans and they don't. Don't take it personally."

"I'm not taking it personally. I'm just thankful that I don't live here with these people with the blank eyes who have no concept whatsoever of what reality really is."

"You are hateful," he said.

"No. Just thankful. Thankful that I don't live here, and thankful that I live where I do. And that I have friends like you and Sue," I said.

Randy smiled.

"You know this place isn't so bad. I like the music. But it does make me feel old," he said referring to the old music.

"Well, you are old, asshole," I said as the chipper waitress returned with our burgers. We dismissed the waitress before we continued our conversation. Randy, ever the keen observer, said, "I get the feeling there is a strong pressure to conform in this town. I can see why you left."

"It wasn't the place to be if you were an artist or a person who spoke your mind. It was frustrating, knowing that New York City is a mere hour away, and this place might as well be on the moon with its conforming conservatism. Especially when I lived here and the way I felt about Vietnam."

Randy's face washed over in sorrow, and he tried to change the subject.

"What's the problem, Ran? You didn't support the war, did you?" I asked, nudging him to the forbidden subject.

"No. But I participated in it, and that has to account for something. I still haven't gotten over it, that's all. Don't push, Sandy, I don't want to talk about it."

"But I do. Every time the subject comes up, you get this strange look on your face, and I can't figure it out. So you went. Big deal. So you came back to a less than enthusiastic crowd. Big deal. You could have come back in a box. At least you made it. What gives?" I pushed.

He rubbed his face with one hand and looked at me. "A lot of people didn't make it back because of me," he whispered. "That's what I have been carrying around all these years. Shit. I was young and stupid, and I led my guys into a death trap. I saw kids blown to bits and even had their guts splattered on me. And it was my fault. I tried to tell myself over and over that there was nothing I could do. It's old stuff and it can't be changed. But I still think about it and it still haunts me. I was allowed to live—unscarred—and they died. It isn't fair. And I have these bad dreams sometimes."

I looked at him and began talking about the way Berkeley was during that period.

"These people are shadows of what thy used to be, Ran. This was just a working-Joe suburb filled with people who escaped the swelter of the city. Back then, most were blue-collar middle class and these houses were reasonably priced. Hell, they commuted to places that made cars for chrissake and worked on assembly lines. Some made their way to the city to work regular jobs. And the blue collar thing to do was go to war. Especially for these people who were first and second generation Americans. Most everybody's parents were from Italy—or at least their grandparents were. So men went to war. It was the honorable thing to do. They had no idea that rich folks were ducking out and going to college. Now look at them. These are all college-educated kids of working Joes who can't understand why the government pulled out before we won. They turned it into a success thing.

"And this place is now considered an upper class town. You have to have succeeded in something to be able to live here. No more people trying to escape Berkeley—just people willing to pay anything to get into Berkeley. Funny how things change. Attitudes change," I said.

"Well, it was the same where I grew up, just outside Malibu," he countered. "I went to war because I was told to go by the government. I was trained for one job and wound up doing another in the fucking jungle where no rules applied. I was nineteen and entrusted with the lives of several guys, and I am left to talk about the mistake that killed them while their names are on a granite wall in Washington.

"Don't you see, Sandy? It means something. Sure, I have bad dreams once in a while. And nothing will ever erase the damage I did to so many lives, but I survived—mental scars and all. And I didn't turn it around to make it look like it was the honorable thing to do. I was young and stupid. Today, I would tell the government to go to hell and refuse to go because I have the wisdom.

"Look at us—you, me, and Sue. Because of your belief in artistic freedom, my belief that the war was wrong, and Sue's belief that there is a place for hardworking blue collars, we wound up where we did. We are soaking up the sun, doing what we want, living at *The Hole*. So you happened to make money doing what you want, that's great. But you live in fucking Homestead, not New York, L.A., or some other posh place. And you share your wealth with us. We have something these vacant-faced success stories don't have. We have our dignity and morals. We don't live to excess.

"So the demons that have haunted you and me turned out to steer us in the right direction. Even Pudge had his demons. But he was just a simple fisherman—something that gave him pleasure."

I looked at Randy in a different light. He was right. Those demons and nightmares were worth what we had. We didn't have to take the New Jersey Transit to New York City and screw people for a living. We weren't one of those hollow-eyed people that eked out a living working for someone else. We weren't the ambitious types that followed the Almighty Dollar. We just lived our lives within a close circle of friends and enjoyed ourselves.

So why was I sitting here drowning myself in rum? Was it because I couldn't change the past? Partially. I wanted to be Invincible Woman who could bring back my beloved father, Alex, and my dearest friend, Pudge. We ate our burgers, listened to the music, and chuckled at the conversations of the neo-working people who would gladly give a limb, a spouse, or a child for success. What a difference twenty-some years can make to a town.

We arrived back at the hotel to find Susan sprawled on the bed eating a pizza, engrossed in a movie.

"You guys drunk?" she asked.

"I wish," I answered.

"So, tell me, how was your brush with the past?"

"Uneventful and disturbing. I hate this shit," I said.

"Don't you think you should call your sister and visit her?" Susan said. She took pleasure in being our counselor and conscience. And she did her job well.

"Randy and I can pick up all the things on Truitt that you'll need, and nobody up here knows us so there won't be any suspicion. Right, Randy?" she said.

Randy nodded in agreement and added, "This is probably the worst part of everything—especially after all he did when you were a kid."

There was no way to argue with them, and I really didn't care about what had happened to Truitt, except I was sorry I wasn't the one who killed him. But, I reminded myself, the reason I am doing this is because of Pudge. As long as I kept Pudge in the forefront of my mind, I could get through all this stuff. I picked up the phone and called Mary. I told her that I would stop by tomorrow and spend the day with her. She sounded happy, I think.

I took a long, hot shower and tried not to think too much. As I settled on the bed, I picked up another of Pudge's journals and read about the beautiful Josephine and the boy again. Funny, but every time Pudge mentioned Josephine, her hair was a different color. She must have been one classy lady, even if she did repeatedly dye her hair. I was dying to find out where the boy was. According to Pudge, he never met the other offspring. Somehow, the boy stood apart. I summed it up that he was a child of the woman Pudge truly loved, and I wanted to find her because if she could hold Pudge's heart in her hands, she was one special person.

Once again, I fell asleep reading Pudge's words. I dreamed that Randy and I were diving in deep water. I checked my depth gauge and it read one-hundred-twenty feet. I looked up and couldn't see the sunlight on the surface, and I looked below and couldn't see the bottom. For a minute, I paused suspended in the water and stretched out on my back not moving. I just hovered, perfectly neutral, in the middle of the water. When I looked for my friend, he was gone. Vanished in the middle of the ocean! I did the logical thing—I started for the top calmly and slowly checking around for any sign of Randy. Suddenly, I was stopped by a familiar pull on my right leg. The snake! Only it wasn't a snake, it was an eel. It was perfectly purple with green eyes and a multitude of razor sharp teeth in its opening and closing mouth—just like the snake. It pulled me lower in the abyss. I checked my depth gauge again and watched as the needle pointed to one hundred twenty-five, then one hundred thirty-five, and one hundred fifty-five. I tried to fill my buoyancy control vest with air to offset the pull of the eel, but it didn't work. My breathing became labored as I tried to fight the monster off. I reached for my knife and figured I could stab it away, but the eel moved suddenly, forcing the knife from my shaking hands, and I watched helplessly as it floated to the depths.

I sensed myself picking up speed as I descended to dangerous levels and felt the pressure build against my lungs. I looked at the eel as if to ask why it was doing this to me, and its green eyes turned into crystal emeralds. My breathing became a real effort now, and just as I was about to slip into unconsciousness, I woke from *The Dream* in a bed of sweat. Pudge's journal was still across my chest. Sitting upright on my bed, blinking into the darkness, I realized I didn't scream or call out this time. I was thankful that I wouldn't have to listen to my friends tell me I needed to see a shrink. I put the journal on the floor beside the bed and lay back down to continue my slumber. This time, my much-needed rest was uninterrupted by *The Dream*, and I slept a restful sleep.

When I woke, Randy and Susan were gone. They left a note saying they took the map and were going about the business of tracking the paper trail Truitt left behind. They took a cab and left me the van. I was thankful that I had such good friends. Hell, I didn't have any other friends except them. I settled for quality, not quantity, insofar as friendship was concerned. Either that or I was a total bitch that nobody could possibly put up with. I dressed and called Mary to let her know I was on my way. Then I took a quick drink of rum, my breakfast, and left the hotel.

Traveling up the mountains to Mary's house conjured pangs of longing. I loved the trees and the mountains, especially in the spring. By the time I pulled into her driveway, however, I reminded myself that the grandest mountains were on Caribbean islands, and the best trees were the tropical type. I longed for a mango and more heat and humidity. Mary was waiting at the door and embraced me like only a sister could. Her house was the usual spotless home that I expected to see and everything was in its place. She inherited that from our mother. *The Hole* looked like what it was called, and whenever I had visitors, I scrambled for a day or two to get it cleaned. Mostly I just shoved everything in the closets or carried it out to the shed. A few years past, I can't recall who said it, but someone said, "I can't understand why your house is always a mess. I mean, you're home all the time. It's not like you actually work or anything."

So, I sat in front of a computer in my home office all day and played? I didn't work? I wish I could remember who said it, but it was probably someone who never sat down for eight hours and tried to write a story. My thoughts were interrupted by my sister's loving voice.

"Are you going to tell me why you're here?" she asked as she led the way to the kitchen.

"I have some business in New York. I have to meet with Paul and go over some things for a new book. Stuff like that," I answered.

"Have you heard from Mom?"

"Yes. I spoke with her last week, and she said she was coming home soon. Then I spoke with Shane, and he said that she would be home next week. I figure I'll get back in time to go over and straighten up her place before she gets back."

"It must be nice living close to Mom," Mary said. She had a faraway look in her eyes.

"It is. Or it was. Now that Dad is gone, she doesn't spend too much time at home. But I do miss going over there and visiting with the two of them," I said.

"Yeah, I really miss Daddy, too. And Alex. I can't believe they are gone. I feel sorry for Mom though. She and Alex really did everything together."

I knew what she was talking about when she said she missed everybody. Mary was so far away from Mom and Alex, she hardly saw them, but at least she knew they were there. But as for missing her father ... well, Carlo could be in the same room, and he still wasn't there. He was the shallowest person I had ever known. But, I was on my best behavior and didn't say anything to Mary who loved him very much. I did feel he was unworthy of her love and hoped she wouldn't canonize him.

Most of the rest of our conversation was about the kids and how much they'd grown. We didn't speak of people I knew when I lived there because Mary knew I never kept in touch with anyone. She said she didn't care for my last book—too many fucks in it—but she was happy it sold well. As she spoke, I studied her face. It was the same beautiful face she had in high school. She was always the pretty one in the family. I was always the one who didn't give a shit what I looked like. When we were younger, I remember her trying to fix my hair. She would put these huge rollers in my hair, tell me to go to sleep, and when I woke, she would comb it out. I would wake to find the rollers on the floor and Mary all pissed at me for taking them out. I didn't remember taking the rollers out. I did it in my sleep. She would paint my nails. I would chip the polish off. She would give me dresses to try on, and I would still walk like I was wearing jeans. And here she was, my older sister, still looking like the prom queen, only better. Childbearing hadn't flawed her perfect figure, and she still turned heads. Me? I was still the carefree slob I always would be. The years of drinking and staying up all night had taken their toll, and I looked a good five years older than my older sister. And my hair still hung straight down to my hips. No fancy coiffures for this head.

"So, tell me, Sandy, is there anyone special in your life? Any prospective husbands?" she asked.

"Not quite. I still fancy one-nighters when the urge hits me," I said, trying to remember the last time I even had sex.

She blushed, smiled, and retorted, "But what about all the diseases out there?"

"I make them fill out a medical report first. Mostly, just guys I know real well. I seldom take on new members," I said jokingly.

"Really?"

"No. Mostly, I just sit around and think about sex. Then I channel my frustration to something else—writing or spearfishing."

"Spearfishing?"

"Hey, it works for me."

"You are strange."

"Yeah, but at least I have a lot of fresh fish at the house."

She laughed.

Four hours had past, and the kids started coming home from school. I talked with them for a while and waited until my brother-in-law came home before I left.

"You're not staying for dinner?" he asked.

"No, I can't really. I have to get back to my hotel room and arrange all my papers for the trip to New York tomorrow. Paul hates it when I come to the office and scatter all these pages across his desk. He finally taught me how to organize the paperwork," I said.

I kissed and hugged everybody, especially Mary.

"Take good care of yourself. I love you," she said.

I left the house feeling a slight bit inadequate. This was what a real family was supposed to be like, and I had nothing even close. But, I couldn't picture myself doing these little family things for very long. And I doubted it would make me happy. So, I concluded, my life is perfect for me, and I wouldn't change it even if I could.

I drove through Berkeley one last time on my way to the motel, stopping at a grocery store for cigarettes and a Coke. I wandered the aisles looking for a bag of potato chips to go with the Coke. Dinner, I thought. I grabbed the two items and cigarettes and headed for the checkout counter taking my place behind two familiar-looking people. I kept my head down, eyes fixed on the floor, and patiently waited. I placed my cigarettes, Coke, and chips on the conveyor and eased my way to the cashier who totaled my dinner.

"Twenty-one seventy," she said.

I looked up and stared into the vacuous eyes of a woman I had gone to school with. She was popular then. Cheerleader material. Now, she had that bored-with-life look in her brown eyes, and her hair was graying.

"Here you go," I said as I handed her a twenty-dollar bill and a five-dollar bill.

"Sandy? Is that you?" she asked.

"Yeah, Katie, it's me. How have you been?" I said trying not to let her know how eager I was to get out of there.

"You still look the same, only tinier than I remember. You still writing? I know a lot of people that read your stuff. I read it too. It's good."

"Thanks."

"Why don't you stick around for a while? There is going to be a small get-together after nine tonight at Park Place. It's my fifteenth anniversary," she said proudly.

"Fifteen years? You mean you've been married fifteen years?" I asked.

"No. Not married. Well, I am married, but it's my third marriage. I've been working here for fifteen years—since school. I never really wanted to go anywhere else," she said.

I nearly gagged.

"Katie," I said as I placed my things in a bag, "I really would love to stay, but I have to get some papers together. I have to be in New York tomorrow morning, and I just stopped by to see my sister. Give my best to everybody who knew me."

"Well, how about when you finish in New York? It'll be great to sit and talk about old times," she nearly pleaded.

"Sorry. I have to get back to Florida. Maybe next time," I said politely.

Two more patrons came to the checkout line, and Katie said a hasty goodbye. I turned and left the grocery store with my bag. I nearly ran across the parking lot to the van and quickly got inside. I was afraid if I strayed too long, I might get stuck here and my whole life would revolve around going to work at a grocery store. Fifteen years at a checkout counter! What aspirations some people have in life. I supposed there really wasn't too much to aspire to in Berkeley, and like I told Randy, there was a stifling wind that blew through this town and made people forget that life existed somewhere else. The residents were raised to please others and to serve. Dreams were for the foolish and selfish. And this foolish, selfish person eased her way onto the main street out of town.

Even the night was a carbon copy of the night before. Nothing ever changed in this cocoon town. Everybody was well insulated from the outside world, and all was well with the people of Berkeley. It was just another spring night, another rebirth of the year. Another chance to do exactly the same thing that had been done last year with the same people. The vision made me truly miss my home in the Redland and my drives to the Keys to Amaretto. I felt my tan begin to fade from lack of adequate tropical sun and told myself if I lived here, not only would my brain stifle, but my skin would probably fall off, too. I suddenly felt closer to my mother and discovered a newfound respect for her. She broke away from here twenty years ago, and although her dreams of becoming an artist were pretty well quashed by the time she left, she handed her dreams to me and made sure I had the opportunity to live a real life. I made a mental note to thank her profusely for getting me out of here when she did and for rescuing me from Marion as well.

The short ride to the motel seemed to take an awful long time, but I finally made it. I took what was left of my dinner into the room and was glad to see Randy and Susan.

"Dinner," I said, holding up the bag. I poured the rest of the Coke in a glass and added enough rum to change the color.

"Want some Coke with that rum, Sandy?" Sue asked.

I grinned and nodded.

"So, how'd it go?" I asked.

Randy pointed to a stack of papers on the desk. "He wasn't squashed like Carlo. He was burned when his car plunged down the ravine and exploded. There was one witness who said he was sure there were out-of-state tags on the car that ran Jack off the road, but the investigation was concluded without a major pursuit. Not too many people liked the guy."

"I can understand that," I said. "He was a real asshole."

"He left all his stuff to his daughter, the one who called you. And there was an investigation several years ago that concerned his fondling a firefighter's daughter, but charges were dropped after the girl, Clair Montenaro, recanted her story," Randy added.

He rubbed his hand over his face in frustration. "Nothing else to go on, Sandy. We have all this shit, and no leads as to who did any of this. I don't think there is anything that ties this to Carlo's demise and nothing at all to Pudge. The MO is different. Carlo was smashed. Truitt was run off the road. The only link is the out-of-state tags."

"Oh, they're related, Randy. I can feel it. But I can't figure out who could have known both of them—other than me. And we know that I didn't do it," I said.

"But," Susan interjected, "I am leaning toward Laura killing Carlo. Especially based on what Christine told you."

"Things are never what they seem," I said and changed the subject to the person I saw in the grocery store. Both my friends couldn't believe that anyone's aspiration could be to forever work as a cashier. Then we turned our plans to the next day and our trip to New York. Randy and Susan would wait for me to get through in Paul's office, and I would show them around the city. They had never been there before and were looking forward to the sights. I told them there were only two requirements I had to fulfill after the literary meeting: a walk across the Brooklyn Bridge and a trip to Ellis Island to see my grandmother's name on the Wall of Immigrants. Walking across the Brooklyn Bridge was my favorite ritual that began when I was in school and used to cut classes. I would go to the Shakespeare in the Park series at Central Park and then head to the bridge afterward and look at the ships passing under the prettiest bridge in the world. The trip to Ellis Island was because one has to pay homage to heritage.

They agreed that would be all right, and we ordered more dinner from room service, even though the chips had pretty much filled me up.

I fell asleep before midnight, awoke at two and poked around on the computer for a couple of hours, and fell back to sleep around four before waking at eight.

Our trip to New York was as grand as most trips to New York. The weather cooperated—clear skies with a few clouds floating aimlessly across the sky and unusually warm temperatures in the low eighties. Spring was in full bloom in Central Park, and the abundance of flowers made up for the tiny leaves on the trees. In another month, the trees would be enveloped in fine greenery providing shade to people seeking refuge from the city heat.

My trip to Paul's office was comforting and predictable. After several years of collaboration, he had come to trust my literary judgment, and he gave me every opportunity to veer off on my own. This time was no exception, and he handed me an advance check for The Book With No Ending. Then my friends and I strolled the city putting about ten miles on our shoes before we headed back to the motel in New Jersey. We stuffed most of our belongings back into the van, did some laundry, and prepared for a quick trip home. We decided to drive furiously—stopping only when necessary to eat or use the restroom—taking turns at the wheel while the other two rested. I was glad that I wasn't the only person suffering homesickness. But for Randy and Susan, the trip home meant more; I had already told Shane to contact the real estate agent handling the sale of the house next door and tell her that I wanted it. Shane said there might be a problem with the sale, but the agent had an idea I might agree to.

When we hit the road, I thought about this whole trip and how little it yielded. I didn't find out who killed Carlo and Jack. And I still didn't know who killed Pudge. But, strange as it seemed, I didn't feel the trip was a waste of time. I got to know my friends better, and the change of scenery made me appreciate Homestead more than I already did. I learned a valuable lesson about home being where the heart, or the heat, is. I also learned that Shane, when left alone, could handle the responsibility of running a home—two homes, counting Mom's home. No, the trip wasn't wasted. It was a rejuvenation, a celebration. After all, the two people I hated most were dead, and I traveled a long distance to see it wasn't just hearsay; I saw my sister, and I even strolled through the house that I spent my childhood in. Now, I was satisfied to return to South Florida, warm weather, *The Hole*, and Amaretto. I was also looking forward to seeing my mother who would be returning a day after I got home. And I told myself *The Dream* would disappear as soon as my head hit my own pillow on my own bed.

Chapter 8

Homecoming

Florida is a long state to get out of, but when you call the southern end of it home and you are returning, it feels endless. Driving at breakneck speed, taking care to watch for cops—I still had the sinking feeling that someone was going to peg the deaths of Truitt and Carlo on me—I took the wheel and made it back to Dade County in record time. I had wings on my wheels trying to get back home and told Susan and Randy that I was going to kiss the ground when I got to *The Hole*. It was late afternoon when I stopped a final time for gas at the north end of the county, and as I opened the door, that familiar blast of sticky humid air hit my face and filled my nostrils. I drew a full breath and savored the smell and the feel. In less than an hour, I pulled up my secluded driveway and was home. I leapt from the van, fell to my knees and kissed the grass like I said I was going to do. Mickey Dog came bounding around the van and knocked me over. For once, my faithful dog was glad to see me. Looking up, I saw my Shane, and he offered me his hand to help me up. We embraced tightly and over his shoulder I noticed a very tall, sleek woman with honey-brown hair that dusted her shoulders. Her brown eyes danced in the sunlight.

"Mom, I want you to meet Donna. Donna this is my mother, Sandy," my son said.

I took the woman's slender hand in mine and welcomed her.

"Shane is always talking about you. You must really be something," she said as she smiled.

I grinned back. "Where did you meet?" I asked.

I am a friend of Mara's. I was visiting her, and she introduced me to Shane."

I suppose I looked like I was going to ask, and Donna sensed it, so she quickly offered, "I'm straight."

Randy and Sue came around the van and were introduced to Donna. Randy followed her every move with his eyes, and I swear I saw him beginning to salivate. I rapped him hard in the ribs and gave him a sharp look. We began unloading the packed van, and Randy began telling Shane how I chased *The Floater* off with a roll of quarters. As a keen observer, I noticed something different about the yard.

There was a bed of flowers where the mud used to pile up around the front of the house, and two arbors were hoisted on either side of the property where a clearing had been swathed through the tangle of Brazilian pepper. The beginnings of hibiscus were nestled at the bases of each arbor. Red brick paths were started on the ground under the flowering arches—one leading toward Mara's house and the other toward the western side of the property.

"Shane?" I asked pointing with both hands. "Excuse me. But what the hell is this? I mean the flowers and the paths? What is going on here?"

"Oh, Mom," he began, "Mara and I decided that you have lived in isolation too long. And there are friends on either side of you now, so you don't have to worry about your precious privacy.

This way, Randy and Sue can just come over without having to travel the road and so can I. Donna and I are moving into the cottage behind Mara's house. And the flowers add a homey touch to *The Hole*, even if you won't keep the inside clean."

"But, I thought the house deal fell through?" I asked and said at the same time.

He winced as he spoke, knowing I would be pissed, but the irony of the situation was I wasn't pissed. I thought it was a good idea. If, in the event someone moved, the arches could be removed and the path dug up. In no time at all, the Brazilian pepper would conceal the path, and I would again be alone. I was glad he decided to do it.

"Any other surprises?" I asked.

"Yes. Grandma is coming home tomorrow. I'll go get her from the airport. And, her house is clean."

So was mine. I noticed as soon as I opened the door. Either Shane had not touched a thing in the house, or he took a quick lesson in housekeeping 101. But, I was still confused about the path.

"Donna and I went over this place like gangbusters," he said proudly.

"I can tell. The only other person who can clean this place like this is Susan. And I don't think she feels up to it," I said as I noticed Sue flopped on the couch, Mickey Dog panting in her face.

"You got that right. Shane, your mother dragged us all over the place. And then, when she wanted to come home, she drove so fast Randy and I were glued to the backs of our seats."

"Shut the fuck up. I got you here alive, didn't I?" I quipped.

"I hate to break up this friendly spar—and yes, Donna, my mother has a mouth like a drunken sailor—but I contacted the real estate person handling the house next door, and Mara knows her, too. There is already a contract on the house. So, Mara got in touch with an architect who would be happy to plan a house on the next acre of your property," my son said.

I looked over at Randy and Sue and nodded in agreement. Why not let them live on my property?

I was beginning to wonder if there was anybody Mara didn't know. As I thought of her, I heard her voice as she entered *The Hole*.

"Hello! Welcome home!" she said as she hugged Randy and made her way to Sue. She was holding a freshly baked pineapple cake in her hand, and it smelled like a multiple orgasm. She approached me and held out her free hand.

"Shane said you hate the touchy-feely type, so here."

I took her hand, and decided what the fuck is one more hug, and I pulled her close. Actually, I wanted to get closer to the pineapple cake. I swear I was getting a rush from the smell.

"I made this for you—sort of a welcome home thing. Do you like the idea of the paths? I told Shane if you didn't like it, we could take it away. And he has been busting his backside planting flowers and taking out weeds. I know how it is when you are busy, so I gave him a bit of help," she said in what seemed like one long breath.

"Gee, Mara, thanks for everything," I said. "And are you sure you want these two to live in your cottage?"

"Why not? We could be one big happy family. We all like our privacy, although none as severely as you, and yet I think we should be close enough to depend on one another. Shane tells me you haven't left the sixties, so you have your own commune here. A lesbian couple, two kids cohabitating, a married straight pair, and you," she said.

"And me. I sort of defy description, I guess," I said.

"Well, you are hard to peg," Mara said.

"How about bitchy middle-aged woman who can't get laid and has a gutter mouth?" Randy said.

"Oh, Randy," Sue interjected, "It's not that she can't get laid. It's that she won't get laid."

"Yeah," I said, "it might change my attitude. And you know I don't want to do that."

"Not to change the subject, but would you like to have some of this cake and coffee? The coffee should be ready. You did start it as soon as they came home, didn't you, Shane?" Mara asked.

Shane nodded.

"That cake smells so good, Mara, I think I could have an affair with it," I said.

"And you wouldn't be disappointed either. I'll give you the recipe," Mara said. I was beginning to like her, and I was glad she moved in next door, even if she did analyze my dreams without my permission. Some things I prefer to keep to myself and dreams are one of them.

"Oh, Mara. I thought you'd just make one every time I wanted one," I said.

"You are a bitch, aren't you? Just like your son said."

"If you'll bake that cake for me, you can call me worse if you like."

We had some cake and coffee and traded light conversation before Randy, Sue, and I went next door and checked the property. It needed to be cleared. And they could put in a swimming pool. If it was on their property, I didn't have to take care of it, but I could use it. When I mentioned the idea, both were in agreement. Randy added that we could get our scuba gear on and sit on the bottom of the deep end for a few hours when we couldn't make it to the sea.

Speaking of sea, I couldn't wait to get to Amaretto. I wanted to get to her now, but I knew I couldn't just get up and leave. There was too much laundry to do and too much unopened mail to tend to. I probably wouldn't make it there tomorrow either, not with my mother coming home. So I settled for the day after. But, oh, how I ached to get back to my beloved Amaretto. Pudge had left me a spell, I told myself, and I was mesmerized with the thought of Amaretto.

After the initial welcome home had died down, I repaired to my office and opened my mail. There was nothing that needed immediate attention, so I called the architect and made an appointment. He would be delighted to draw out the plans. I wanted it, as is, in cash. Delighted. I hated that fucking word.

I went to my room and undressed. What I really wanted was a shower in my own bathroom. I stood outside the stall waiting for the hot water to arrive and fingered the golden anchor on the chain around my neck. I felt like I let Pudge down by not finding out who killed him. And I felt like a fool for traveling all those miles for nothing. A wave of exhaustion fell over me, and as soon as I stepped from the shower, I toweled dry and fell across my bed.

I had *The Dream* again and woke suddenly. I stayed in my room until I was sure there were no effects of the nightmare remaining on my face. Things had quieted down considerably at *The Hole*. Randy and Sue were resting in their room, and Shane and Donna were not there. I fixed a cup of coffee and took Mickey Dog out with me to the patio.

Summer had arrived early this year. The air was laden with moisture, and the ground was wet following the brief storm I slept through. I could hear thunder rumbling in the distance and watched the muted bursts of lightning on the evening sky. Dusk was here and the rain had passed. The doves began their evening chant, and a lone squirrel scurried across the yard piquing Mickey's interest for a fleeting second. My eyes came to rest on the mango tree, and I noticed the fruit was much bigger than this time last year. I couldn't wait for the fruit to ripen. I bet mango would make for a great cake, I thought. I decided to stroll the new path and see where Shane and Donna had taken up residence. The cottage sat at the back of Mara's property and consisted of one large living room, a small kitchen, a bathroom, and one bedroom. There were flower boxes on the windowsills. Mara had a thing about flowers, I decided. I knocked gently and Shane opened the door.

"You're curiosity finally got to you," he said.

"Well, I just want to see where my son is living, that's all."

Donna emerged from the bedroom and they showed me the whole place, which took about two minutes. It was pleasant enough, and I was happy that Shane would remain close to *The Hole*.

"Hey, Mom. You didn't get to meet Mara's girlfriend, Anna, did you?" Shane asked.

"No. She wasn't at *The Hole* when we got back, was she? If she was, I missed her."

Donna looked at Shane and said, "Anna didn't get here until after your mother went to her room."

"Oh, yeah, that's right. Sorry. Anyway, Mom, she is really nice. I'm sure you will meet her soon," he said.

"Well, I'm looking forward to it, Shane," I said in my polite, motherly voice. "Now, I really need to get back home. There is no end to the laundry. What time is Grandma coming in tomorrow?"

"Early. About six or seven. Don't worry, we'll get her and take her home. You can see her when you wake up," he said. Shane knew how I positively despised forced early wake ups. If my eyes opened at five, that was fine, I could handle it. But, if I had to set an alarm clock to awaken at six or seven, I was pretty well useless for the rest of the day.

"Well, Kid, I better get a move on. It was nice seeing your place," I said as I backed out of the door.

I made my way toward the path when the breeze picked up from the east carrying soft, passionate moans from Mara's open window. I picked up my pace just in case they heard my footsteps; the last thing I wanted was for them to think I was listening to them. I disappeared into the bushes and thought how there seemed to be somebody for everyone else in the world but me. I felt lonely for the first time since right after Lee decided to leave. I swept the emotion from my brain before I returned to my porch and took my place beside Mickey.

As darkness swept across the yard, a feeling of regret came over me. I had never told Pudge just how much he meant to me. I had given much thought to my feelings for him during the trip, and I realized that I could have fallen in love with the old fisherman, if I gave myself half a chance. But I had to always be so in charge of my emotions at all times that I couldn't bring myself to tell anyone I loved them. Now, Pudge was gone, and I would never have the chance to at least let him know I wanted to give it a try. I felt tears sting my face as I thought of him. I could almost see his dancing blue eyes and his gray-flecked black hair tucked neatly under his cap. Certainly, I could have meant as much to him as his Josephine did if I had opened my mouth and told him how I felt. I rubbed away the tears and told myself that Pudge was gone, and it probably wouldn't have worked out anyway. He'd have laughed at me if I told him that I was in love with him. I could almost hear him say, "You're too young and lively to be in love with an old fisherman."

In any event, I felt that Josephine was quite a lady, and I was a salty old witch.

It may have taken me three days, but I was on my way to my beloved Amaretto for the first time since I returned home. I spent the last few days organizing my notes, getting ready to begin the new book, and when I wasn't working, I was at my mother's house. She had returned from France well rested and happy, although there was still an empty space where Alex used to be. Everywhere I turned in Mom's house, I saw my dad. I missed him terribly and seeing her without him only amplified his absence. We spent almost an entire day gossiping about the people in Berkeley. And I did thank her for getting me out of there. I asked several questions about Truitt, and Mom said he was a good man—she didn't know what he did to me—but he had a mean streak, and Jack probably made someone mad enough to kill him. I didn't mention all the stolen items Clancy sent me. As for Carlo, mother could think of no good words for him, but she was happy that Christine was planted firmly in place doling out punishment on Laura. She laughed when I told her that Laura was now a waitress, and her daughter was the one who forced Carlo out of his social standing. Still, she said, she thought the person who was hurt most by everything was my sister, Mary. How Mary loved her father! But, I told my mother, Mary loves everybody and takes everything to heart. One day, she'll realize that this world is filled with rotten people that aren't worth the time and energy to love.

I thought of my mother as I headed south to Amaretto. She was a strong and determined person. Maybe I took after her, but my strength needed a boost from rum now and then. I had loaded up the van with Pudge's journals that I had taken with me on the trip. I was going to replace them and start on another set as soon as I hit the deck. The cold chill that rushed across me the last time I set foot on Amaretto was but a fleeting memory. If she were haunted, that spirit would have to put up with me. It would be a battle of nerves, and I was wagering on myself to win. People don't scare me when they're alive, and I'd be damned if I'd let a fucking ghost scare me. If I couldn't see it, then it simply didn't exist. A smile crossed my face when I recalled the look on Harve's face when he told me about the boat being haunted. Too long at sea, I thought. Harve has been off solid ground for too long.

I pulled up to the dock and saw my Amaretto bobbing gently on the incoming tide. She looked finer than I remembered. This was my castle. Harve was on the dock spinning yarns with the other shrimpers, and when he saw me coming, he waved furiously in my direction.

"See any more ghosts, Harve?" I asked.

"You ought not to be making fun of ghosts, Sandy. Nope. I ain't seen no more," he said.

"That's because I took them with me," I said to his smiling face.

He told me that Amaretto had been no problem, and nothing weird had happened since I was gone—no cold wind and no people wandering her decks. I reached in the back of the van and pulled out a wooden case.

"What's that? Here let me give you a hand," Harve said.

"Just hold on a minute, Harve," I said as I set the box on a cooler. "Here, this is for you and the guys. For watching Amaretto."

I pried the top open and revealed twenty-four bottles of twelve-year-old scotch. Harve's eyes bulged in excitement, and he called the other fishermen over.

"Sandy, you didn't have to do this," he said.

"I know, but you guys are all I have left of Pudge, man. I have to be good to you. You're all going to let me come out and haul 'em in with you soon, right?" I winked and they all nodded.

Dave piped up that there was no better woman for the job, and they were all sure that I could handle it as long as I got the right crew. Randy came to my mind.

"You playin' poker with us tonight? We got rum, you know," Harve said.

I smiled. "No. I have to get Amaretto cleaned up. I want to clean up the nets, steady the outriggers, and get her ready for a trip—not a fishing trip—just a trip. I need to get away from fucking land."

"You going out alone? That may not be smart," Harve offered.

"Harve, look at me. Look at Amaretto. Who is going to fuck with a bitch on an old broken down fishy-smelling boat? It ain't like I reek of money here. And there ain't no drugs on board. And Amaretto ain't up to outrunning the Coast Guard. So what could possibly go wrong?"

"Absolutely nothing, Sandy. I just keep forgetting who I'm dealing with. I sometimes think you're a normal woman, that's all," he said.

With that, he patted my shoulder and gave me a hand with the journals. He placed them on Amaretto's deck and asked if I needed help with anything. I told him I didn't and dismissed him to drink scotch with his friends. I had a feeling there was going to be some serious scotch drinking by the time night rolled around.

Everything was just how I had left it. This time, there was nothing moved on Pudge's bunk; his ashes were still in the same place. I poured myself a water glass of warm rum and began arranging the journals on the shelf. A soft breeze swept through Amaretto's insides carrying the fresh smell of salt. The odor of pipe tobacco still lingered in the air after all this time, and Pudge's presence was close at hand; I could feel it. But, it wasn't scary. It was comforting. I made a list of provisions I would need, and as I sat on the bunk, I wondered how I would break the news to Randy and Susan that I would be leaving for a while. My mind hadn't been made up about leaving until I set foot on Amaretto, but now I was sure that I could get a lot more writing done if I was alone at sea.

I drained the glass of rum and picked up the most recent of Pudge's journals. The back pages were blank, not yet filled in. I placed his cap on my head, propped the journal on my knees, and began to read until Pudge's words, the sea air, and the gentle rocking of Amaretto lulled me to sleep.

Once again, I was in the water with that evil-eyed eel pulling me down, and I fought it with a vengeance. Again, I lost my knife trying to kill it. This time, I did reach out with both hands and caught the monster behind its head. I squeezed with all my strength trying to kill the demon, but its gaping grin became hysterical laughter, and its green eyes popped out of their sockets revealing a large cache of emeralds. I forced my eyes open and bolted upright on the bunk throwing the journal to the floor. When I caught my breath, I reached for the book—its pages bent and scattered under the binding—and pulled it up. A tiny scrap remained on the floor and I retrieved it. The writing on the back was faded pencil and read "Billy Barrington Aug. 12, 1958." I turned it over and studied the faded, creased photo a long time. I carried it to the table in the galley and turned on the overhead light for a better look. My blood ran cold, and I couldn't believe what I was seeing.

Standing next to a boat, not Amaretto, was a slender young man with liquid crystal blue eyes. His hair was a thick mass of raven curls and his body so lithe it was as if he was standing six inches above the ground. There was that familiar smile though. The smile distinguished the person as Pudge, but he looked more like *The Floater* than my old friend. That cold chill swept through Amaretto again, and I knew I wasn't alone. This time, the chill chased me from her decks, and I shoved the photo in my pocket as I nearly ran toward the van. I closed the door and listened to my own rasping breath as I forced air in and out of my lungs. A sour nausea was about to erupt from the pit of my stomach, and I knew I had to do something about *The Dream, The Floater*, and the cold wind. Turning the key, I decided I was going to do what I should have done a long time ago—visit *The Moon Lady* to find out what my dreams were about. And I hoped Bill the Floater was there, too; I had a lot of questions.

The early evening sun, a giant red-orange globe, was making it's final call on the horizon as I pulled the van into the parking lot of the No Name. There were no other vehicles in the lot. Mostly all the tourists had gone by this time, especially since the summer pattern weather had made an early return. But I could hear the voices of the local patrons from the parking lot. I felt secure in knowing I wasn't going to be alone in this strange place.

As I entered the bar, I saw *The Moon Lady* right away. She had a purple and red paisley muumuu on, several pieces of gaudy jewelry, and a green silk scarf wrapped around her head. She glared at me as I approached her table.

"Ma'am, I need to talk with you," I whispered as I stood beside the chair opposite her and waited for an invitation.

"Now you want to talk? I thought you didn't believe. You have all the answers, remember?" she said.

"Look, I'm sorry for what happened the last time I was here. Really. I need to talk with you. I keep having this dream. Please," I said, nearly whining for an invitation to sit down.

She reached up and removed her scarf, revealing flaming orange-red hair piled loosely on top of her round head. She didn't have nearly as much makeup on as she did the last time I was here. *The Moon Lady* pointed to the chair beside me and motioned for me to sit.

"Tell me about the dream," she said softly.

I ordered a rum and began telling her about the snake and the eel and how the damned thing kept pulling me down into an abyss, and I couldn't fight it off. I told her my neighbor said it was sexual, but I didn't think so. She listened with interest as I described the emeralds falling from the serpent's eyes. I told *The Moon Lady* that I haven't had a good night's sleep since *The Dream* became more intense, and it was driving me crazy. I couldn't drink it away, and I had no control over when it would come.

She reached into a leather bag and pulled out two shiny stones and four shells. Tossing them on the table, she began a soft chant and her eyes rolled back into her head. Personally, I was mortified and about to get up and get the hell out of that place. Before I could move, *The Moon Lady* returned to normal, or what passed for normal for her, and reached across the table to take my hands. She squeezed them, looked into my eyes, and spoke very slowly and softly.

"To get rid of your dreams, you must understand them. But you always fight them because they are not reality and frightening. Follow your dream," she said. "See where the dream leads. The snake could be a great leader trying to tell you something. Do not force yourself awake. Follow the dream, and you will find answers."

Then she let go of my hand, sat back in her chair, and smiled at me.

"Are you scared?" she asked.

"Well, I'm not exactly jumping for joy here. What if I can't find my way back?" I asked.

"You have the power to get back. Don't worry. Just go. Follow. And come back when you have the answer," she said as she handed me a small vial and told me to drink it before retiring tonight. Then she quickly dismissed me before telling me what was in the bottle.

I tried to give her a twenty, but she smiled and wouldn't take it. I scanned the bar one last time looking for Billy the Floater, but I found no sign of him. I had to see his face again to confirm what I thought—he was Pudge's son—*the boy* my friend wrote about in his journals. I had to find him so I could find Josephine. Shit! The more I discovered, the more I found there was to discover! I raced back to Amaretto and reached into my pocket to make sure the photo was still there. I was determined not to lose it and vowed to keep it with me at all times.

It was almost ten when I decided to call Randy and tell him I went to see *The Moon Lady*. He was amused that I did what I did and asked if I wanted him to come to Amaretto to spend the night with me. I declined the offer and told him to be here in the morning with Sue, because if I had *The Dream* and found out anything, I was hitting the road again. He was not ready to make another excursion for answers, but he soothed me just the same. After I hung up, I realized I didn't tell him about the photo, but I made a mental note to show it to him in the morning.

I extinguished all of Amaretto's lights save the lantern next to the bunk, and I crawled under the covers, pulling them tightly around my neck. The vial was on the stand next to me, and I thought about drinking it, but changed my mind. I closed my eyes and listened to the drunken poker game on Harve's boat. They were enjoying the scotch, I thought, and I was lying here trying to decide if I should drink a bottle of something some old witch lady gave me. I reached through the darkness for the vial and uncapped it. Holding it under my nose to smell it, I was ready to wince. But the aroma was pleasant, sort of like honeysuckle. I ran a cautious finger around the lip of the vial and placed it on my tongue. It tasted sweet. I gazed around the cabin one time, said a silent prayer to Pudge asking him to watch over me and to forgive me for being so gullible, took the entire contents of the vial in my mouth, and swallowed hard.

I don't remember going to sleep, but I know I was sleeping when the snake appeared around my right leg. I was on an island and it pulled me toward the water before letting go. As soon as it released its hold, *The Eel* came and pulled me through the water. The next thing I remember, I was in familiar water over Molasses Reef. The purple sea serpent pulled me down to the reef and held me fast so I couldn't break free. I tried to yank my leg away, but I couldn't free myself. I heard laughter and looked around, but saw nobody.

Playing cards came falling through the water and danced around my head like tropical fish. The queen of hearts landed right side up on the sand just beneath a small jut coming out of the reef. The Eel kept its hold on my leg and pulled me toward the card. I reached out to grab it with both hands; I wanted to kill it, but I couldn't keep my hands on the creature. The grip around my leg grew tighter, and I felt my foot tingle from lack of circulation.

When we were barely a foot above the sand, *The Eel* relaxed its grip and straightened out like a giant purple arrow and pointed its head at the queen of hearts. I looked at *The Eel,* and then at the card, and traced my gaze with my hand. I gently lifted the card from the sandy bottom and stirred the silt free. Something red caught my eye, and I began to dig rapidly in the sand. It was then that I realized I wasn't wearing any scuba gear, and I was breathing under the water! Afraid to take my eyes off the object of my desire, I paid no heed to the tapping at my back. I felt a hand reach across my face and it held a regulator. The hand placed it in my mouth as I continued to unearth a small box—*The Rosewood Box* that had disappeared from Amaretto's hold!

I pulled the box free and set it on top of the sand. Opening it, I felt my heart pounding uncontrollably within my chest, and I noticed the bubbles expelling from my regulator in giant bursts. Carefully, I opened the latch, and there, inside the precious box, were all the emeralds and gold coins Pudge and I had placed in it before hiding it in Amaretto's hold. There was something else there, too—a waterproof logbook with writing on it. But I couldn't make out the words. Only after I resealed the box did I look up and see it was Randy who was with me, and he was the one who placed the regulator in my mouth. I jerked my head from side to side trying to find *The Eel* and saw it to my left—its mouth opening and closing in rhythmic intervals. I stared at those green eyes and they turned to blue, a watery crystal blue, like Pudge's and Billy the Floater's eyes. In a quick flash of light, it disappeared leaving behind a shadow. Following the shadow, I saw it was a shark. But not a real shark—a wooden shark like the one that hung over Mark Chaney's office door. I blinked and it was gone.

Placing the box under my arm, I began to slowly ascend to the surface. When I broke free of the water, my dream turned to darkness, and for the remainder of my sleep, I dreamed nothing.

When I woke, dawn was already breaking over the water. I groped my way to the galley and brewed a pot of coffee. I sat at the table and listened to the silence of the dock. When the coffee was ready, I poured a cup and brought it topside. For a long time, I watched the other fishing boats bob in the water and listened to the intermittent sound of bilge pumps as they expelled water. I remembered my dream in minute detail and was relaxed and well rested. From the parking lot, I heard the sound of tires grinding on the gravel and turned to see it was Randy and Susan.

They boarded Amaretto and looked at me for a long time before Susan spoke.

"You look like you have been sleeping for a week. I don't think I ever saw you so relaxed!"

"Must have been the voodoo stuff *The Moon Lady* gave me," I said.

"Voodoo stuff? What are you talking about?" she asked.

"I don't know what it was, but it put me to sleep. And I had *The Dream*. And I know what it means. And, sorry to inform you, it has nothing to do with sex, Kid," I said to Susan.

"What does it mean?" Randy asked as he emerged from the galley with a cup of coffee.

"It means we're going diving today, Ran. I need to recover *The Rosewood Box*."

My friends said nothing, but they stared at each other a long time as if they were pondering having me committed. I reached into my pocket and pulled out the photo of Pudge and showed it to Sandy.

"Look familiar?" I asked.

"Jesus Christ! It's *The Floater*!" she said.

"No shit. Show it to Randy," I said as I went about getting Amaretto ready for the trip to Molasses Reef.

"You think Bill is the one who Pudge is always referring to as 'the boy' when he writes of Josephine?" Randy asked.

"I believe so. Now, all I have to do is find out who the fuck Josephine is, and I'll be all set."

"You know what I hate?" Randy asked. "I hate it when you have all the answers. You act like wherever it is we are going, we are going to find all the things we need to know."

"You are so fucking perceptive, Friend," I snipped.

"Well, where are we going?" he asked.

"Molasses Reef," I said.

"It is an unlikely dive vessel," Sue said as she looked around.

"Hey, I don't give a shit what it looks like—it gets the job done."

"I suppose you're right," she said as she went below to check our gear and tally the contents of the cooler.

Chapter 9

The Dive

We shoved off within the hour with Amaretto belching black smoke behind. The old girl groaned as we set out toward the reef over seas that peaked at two feet. As I steered Amaretto along our carefully plotted course, I realized it was the first time the old boat had been out on open water since Pudge died. I handed the wheel to Randy and I went below. I retrieved the box of Pudge's remains and brought it to the wheelhouse with me and took over from Randy.

Susan had stripped down to her bathing suit and was basking on the foredeck as we slowed and approached the reef. Randy got me close enough to a mooring ball, and I snagged it with one swipe of the boathook. Carefully, I secured the line to the Sampson post. Randy cut the power to Amaretto as Susan raised the dive flag. We drew curious stares from another vessel in the area, a charter dive boat, but we largely ignored the remarks as we lowered the platform Pudge had constructed for us a while back.

"You ready?" Randy asked as he gave a final check to his gear.

"Whenever," I said as I secured all my hoses.

As we donned our gear, we commented on what a pleasure it was to dive in such calm weather. Amaretto barely rocked on the flat sea, and the sun beamed down on us from a cloudless sky.

Susan came and checked our gear for us as we stood near the side. Then Randy and I gave her a quick thumbs up before we disappeared over the edge of Amaretto into the familiar water above Molasses Reef.

I forced myself to descend slowly, even though I was in a hurry to get to the jut on the reef. Randy didn't even watch where he was going. He kept his eyes glued on me as though I might disappear if he looked away. We made our way down, taking note that the water was unusually clear. We could see the divers from the other boat, and I estimated they were two-hundred feet away. I swam around the reef looking for the jut. I was sure I would recognize it if I saw it. I felt Randy rap me on the arm, and I turned to see what he wanted. He pointed ahead, along the reef. There, as if on guard, was a bright purple eel about ten feet long. Beneath the eel was the jut I was looking for. At that point, I had to remind myself to keep breathing as I crept closer to the eel. When we arrived at the jut, the skittish eel tucked itself neatly into a hole in the reef so just its head was sticking out. Its opening and closing mouth revealed rows of razor sharp teeth, and Randy looked at it with mild fascination. I trained my eyes on a path down from the jut and could see nothing that would indicate where I should begin my search. I hovered above the bottom, being careful not to disturb the sand and occlude my vision. Randy tried to assist me in the search, but he had no idea what he was looking for.

Suddenly, with the quickness of a flash of lightning, the eel flew out of its hole and dipped down between Randy and me, stirring up the sand. Just as quickly, the eel vanished in the clear water giving us no indication in which direction it went. I heard a slight audible gasp escape Randy's regulator, and I followed his pointed finger to the sand below.

Not two feet from my face, embossed in the sand, was the queen of hearts. I touched the magnificent sand sculpture gently, and it powdered under the slightest pressure. Feverishly, I began to fan the bottom until I saw the top of the box. Looking up at Randy's face, I could see he was in a near state of shock. I grabbed my treasure, and as soon as I had it firmly in my grasp, a strong current rushed by and covered the pit I had unearthed. We slowly made our way back to Amaretto without opening the box. Before we broke the surface, I checked all around for any sign of the eel, but it had disappeared. We pulled ourselves up the ladder to the platform where Sue waited to assist us. I carefully handed her the box before getting out of the water.

"If you told me what I was going to see, I would have told you that you were the fucking craziest person in the world!" Randy said as he grabbed my arm for me to lift him from the water."

"Is this the box?" Sue asked.

"Yes." I answered.

"The box isn't half the story, Sue. You had to have seen the sculpture of the queen of hearts down there. And the purple eel. It was absolutely amazing!" her husband exclaimed.

Without another word, I headed to the cabin, set the unopened box on the table, and unsealed the latch. Every single one of the emeralds and the coins were there, just as they were in the dream and so was the waterproof booklet. I left the jewels for Susan and Randy to gaggle over and took the booklet to a chair. Carefully, I wiped it with a towel and opened it to read its contents. In Pudge's handwriting was the following message:

Sandy,

I suppose you are pretty tired from your journey by now. I know you and your suspicious nature too well. You think I was murdered. Well, it isn't true. I killed myself, but only because I had to. You see, an old fisherman is a wise fisherman, and he knows when he's cast his last net upon the open sea. Because of the life I have led, I fell victim to a hideous creature that goes by the name of terminal liver cancer. I couldn't bear to be locked up in a hospital being probed and stuck and drugged like some kind of laboratory rat. No ma'am, they ain't gonna pluck away at ol' Pudge. I knew how much time I had left by the pain in my side, and when it got too bad, I settled my own score on my own terms. However, there are a few things I have left to tell you, my dear friend Sandy, and I apologize for not being able to tell you these things in person. When we used to sit on Amaretto in the moonlight, drinking and confiding, you said a few things that remained with me. One was that you suffered terribly at the hands of two men. One shattered your childhood with his abuse, and the other shattered your faith with his selfishness. Ah, hell, if I had been braver, I would have been able to tell you how much I loved you and wanted to make it better, but I couldn't. What would you want with an old shrimper with a shady past?

I decided that since I was going to die, I might as well erase those unpleasant memories for you. I employed my son to hunt down and remove Carlo Anitelli and Jack Truitt so they could never haunt you again. You thought I only had daughters, didn't you? Well, they were a legitimate product of my marriage, and I never really had too much to do with them. But, the boy, Bill, was born twenty years ago to a beautiful, mysterious woman named Josephine. She asked nothing from me and was always there when I needed companionship. And she did a fine job raising the boy, despite her strange and mystical ways.

I told my Billy to look after you, because we both know that you have a hard time doing that for yourself—no matter how much you deny it. So don't fret if you see the dark-haired boy on your tail. And go easy on him. Don't try killing him or anything. He hid the rosewood box for me in a place I remember well. It was the first place we were anchored on Amaretto that I realized how very much I loved you and your carefree ways. But I knew you could never love me back, so I said nothing. I just left you all my things in hopes you'd be a little happier in knowing that a true love does exist.

Mark Chaney is the only other person, besides Billy and Josephine, that knows all this, and I made him swear he wouldn't tell you anything. You had to find it out for yourself.

I guess that's about all I have to say, pretty lady, except I hope your life is happier now that the demons are gone. And I will always be close to you—especially when you are sailing Amaretto on the open sea or thinking up a new name for a person as I know you love to do. You are a jewel on the earth, and I hope you have a wonderful life. I am glad I was a part of it. Remember to give my regards to Randy and Susan and share some of what I have left you with them because they are good folks. And, before I close, watch out when you are playing poker with Harve. He cheats.

Take care of yourself, my love, and cast a net out for me once in a while, and I will make sure it comes back full.

All my love,
Pudge.

By the time I finished reading the note, I was crying so hard I couldn't talk. I just handed the booklet to Susan and Randy to read as I sat there sobbing like a child. The tears flowed endlessly, and Randy came to me and held me tightly against his chest as my body heaved with each sob. I cried until I was exhausted and my body ached. Susan and Randy guided me to the forward hatch cover where I stretched out and clutched a towel near my face until I fell asleep still sobbing.

I awoke and we were back at the dock, Amaretto returned to her slip like a queen to her throne. I could hear Randy and Susan talking softly in the wheelhouse, but I wasn't ready to get up and face them yet. I sat up on the deck and blinked as I stared around me at Amaretto's deck. He did love me. Just like I loved him, but we were both too pigheaded to do anything about it. We both thought the other would never take it seriously. And now I lost the only man that I could ever even possibly love. I felt so empty and hollow. But I knew that Pudge didn't tell me because he wanted me to live my own life and not change my ways. He loved me for what I was—more than any other man would ever do. And I respected his decision to take his life. I had no choice but to give him a fitting sendoff like I promised Chaney I would do. I mustered all my remaining strength and walked proudly into the wheelhouse to tell Randy and Susan we had a funeral to plan.

"I am going to the No Name," I announced, "to ask Billy to come here for the service. You want to come with me?"

"Sure. And I think you best apologize to him for almost killing him with that roll of quarters," Randy answered as Susan nodded.

We headed south under the full moon and didn't say a word until we reached the bar on No Name Key.

Coming into the bar from the darkness was a pleasure; it took no time for my eyes to adjust. There were seven patrons listening to the jukebox in the corner, and I saw the back of Billy's head at *The Moon Lady's* table. With my shoulders back and my red-rimmed eyes blinking, I walked proudly to the two of them and stood there searching for the right salutation.

Billy turned his head upward and gazed at me with those blue eyes and said, "You're not carrying a load of quarters, are you?"

I couldn't quell the smile. "No," I answered, "no quarters."

The Moon Lady looked at us quizzically and removed her scarf revealing jet-black hair that fell loosely around her shoulders. She wore no makeup and was quite a pretty woman.

"My father said you were a tough cookie," he said, "but until you tried to shoot me, I had no idea how tough you really were. By the way, I'd like you to meet my mother, Josephine."

He pointed at *The Moon Lady* and she smiled up at me.

Josephine! At last!

"Honey, we already met. The potion worked, I take it?" she asked.

I nodded. "It sure did. Thank you."

From outside on the dock, another familiar face emerged. It was Mark Chaney—*The Shark*.

"Hello, Sandy. How are you?" he asked and then turned his attention to Randy and Susan.

"Can I get you a drink?" the bartender called to me.

"Yes, a Coke, please. Just a Coke," I said as I took a seat next to Billy.

"You guys really pulled one over on me, you know," I said.

"Not us, my father," Billy retorted, "I asked no questions and can only surmise he had his reasons."

"Of course, he did, Billy. He loved her. Even I knew that," Josephine added.

All I could do was smile. Randy and Susan sat next to me, and we told the three of them that we planned to have a memorial service for Pudge off the stern of Amaretto in two days. We wanted them to be there. They all agreed they would come up for the occasion, and we filled the remainder of the moonlit night at the bar with laughter and stories of Pudge and Amaretto.

Chapter 10

Fair Winds and Following Seas

Susan, Randy, and I bumped into each other at least half a dozen times as we struggled to get ready to head to Amaretto for the memorial service. Mickey Dog was busy making sure we tripped over him at every turn. I had decided to take him along because I was planning to renew my friendship with him, and he was going to accompany me on my excursion to the Caribbean. My mother thought I was crazy embarking on a trip like that alone, but I reassured her that I would make daily contacts with either her or one of my friends while I was gone. And I needed to get out on the open water to write this book, which finally had an ending. I had already loaded my computer and notes into the van along with all my other provisions.

Shane appeared in the living room dressed in a clean white shirt and a new pair of jeans. Donna was dressed in a simple white summer dress.

"Mara and Anna are waiting in the car with Grandma. We'll follow you to Amaretto, if you ever got ready," he said.

"Well, I think I am about ready, Shane. Come on, Mickey, we're breaking outta here," I said as I grabbed the last bag that I needed.

Susan and Randy rode with Mickey and me in the van and assured me they would take care of *The Hole* while I was gone. *The Hole*, newly opened by the paths, was safer now from strangers because either of my trusted friends would be able to hear any intruders.

A crew was already clearing the land for Randy and Susan's new home. I smiled at the thought of having neighbors on either side of me.

As we neared the dock, I could see Josephine, Billy, and Mark mingling with Dave, Harve, and the other shrimpers around Amaretto. Harve was holding a bundle of white flowers. I don't know how he comes up with flowers all the time, but he does. I smiled at the thought of him cheating at poker.

Josephine's hair was back to platinum and pulled tightly up on her head, but she wasn't wearing a muumuu this day. She was wearing a white suit with black polka dots and carried a white parasol. We piled out of our vehicles, and I asked that everybody stay off Amaretto until I got my gear loaded up. They didn't argue, and I opened a cooler and invited all to help themselves to Cokes and beer. When we boarded Amaretto, Susan instructed those who weren't familiar with a fishing boat where to sit and to hold on in case we hit choppy seas. Randy called the weather service and was assured we wouldn't be rained on. The seas were running about two to four feet, and the gentle swells lifted Amaretto and her passengers slowly and steadily. We made good time getting to Molasses Reef where we moored and bobbed a while on the water in the searing heat.

"A good day to say goodbye," Billy said as he handed me a Coke.

"Absolutely perfect weather," Josephine said.

Mara and Anna held hands as Randy made the announcement that we were ready to begin our memorial to Pudge. Dave and Harve just stared at the two women and nudged each other.

"My friends and family," I began, "I have had two days to think of something to say that would forever remain in our memories and hearts regarding our friend, Pudge, but for the first time in my life, words escape me. So I chose to read something that Pudge wrote in one of his journals after a particularly rough night of fishing. It goes like this:

Some people were meant to travel the road
And some people were meant to stay at home. Me?
I was meant to travel the sea.
She has been my lover, my friend and my soul
for so long now I couldn't dream of a life without her.
She gives me strength and keeps me in line especially when she tosses and turns
and forces me to my knees when she rages and churns.
But I love her so and I guess I'll stay
for only a fool would turn away from her beauty and bounty
when she is at ease
and the way she clings to my heart
No one could possibly know
The love the lady sea gives me
When I am alone on my Amaretto.

"And now, Pudge, old friend, I will return you to where you belong. Wave to me now and then when I am on the open water. I'll be looking for you, old buddy."

I raised the open box of ashes and spilled them over Amaretto's stern. The cloud remained suspended in the air for a few seconds before falling to the water in a swirl of brown and gray. We all stood there watching, and Harve grabbed his flowers and tossed them in the midst of the swirling remains. We stood in silence for a minute, and Dave broke out a bottle of scotch.

"Take a sip, for ol' Pudge," he said as he passed it around. And we all did. Mickey Dog let out a single bark in memory of Pudge, and we laughed at his perception. Randy started Amaretto, and we headed back to the dock.

Everybody made their way from Amaretto shaking hands and hugging each other. Mara and Anna wished me luck and left first. Then Josephine, Billy, and Mark left, but not before Josephine handed me a thin leather strap with seeds strung on it. "For luck," she said as she placed it around my neck with the golden anchor Pudge had given me.

Shane, Donna, and my mother kissed me goodbye and made me promise to keep in touch. Harve and company gave me last minute pointers on what to do if I saw a large school of fish; I didn't have the heart to tell them that I wasn't going to be doing much fishing this time around.

I boarded Amaretto with Susan and Randy, and we went over my checklist again.

"You sure you want to do this?" Randy asked.

"Why? You want to come with me?" I asked.

"I don't think I could handle another trip with you just yet. I need time to recover from the last one," he said.

"Fuck you, Randy," I quipped.

"Fuck both of you," Sue added shaking her head, "always quibbling, you two. I don't know why I put up with it."

"Because you love us, that's why," Randy said to his wife.

"Really, Randy, I can handle this. No more bad dreams and very little rum. I won't say I'll give it up completely, but I'll definitely cut down," I said.

"I know you can handle the sea, but I don't want to lose you. You're too good a friend," he said.

"I'm touched, Ran. Now don't go getting all misty-eyed on me. I cried enough the night I found Pudge's last journal. By the way, you got the emeralds and coins?" I asked, suddenly remembering I gave the box to Randy.

"Yep, put it in a safe place—the bank safety deposit box," he answered.

"You call a fucking bank safe? You are an asshole!"

"Well, it's better than burying it in the yard for chrissake."

Sue had had enough. "Shut up! Both of you! It'll be fine, Sandy, I'll make sure of it. Now, come on, Randy, let's go home. I'm exhausted."

We hugged and kissed, and they stepped off Amaretto and stood on the dock with Dave and Harve.

I started Amaretto and listened to her finely tuned glub, glub, as she idled in place. Randy untied her and threw the lines to me. I made my way to the cramped wheelhouse, Mickey Dog by my side, and eased her out of the slip and away from the dock without looking back.

When I was about four miles out of port, I turned my head to watch the diminishing coast as it sank over the horizon. I had a good feeling about this trip and an even better feeling about the book. Nothing to distract me but the open ocean and Mickey Dog.

I was jolted out of my solace by the crackle of Amaretto's radio. It was Randy calling from Harve's boat.

"Good luck, sailor, and remember, no more demons."

"Right, Friend," I replied, "no more demons."

I eased up on the throttle, set the automatic pilot, and stood by the starboard rail a minute, just basking in the light. My eyes caught a faint purple vision just below the surface of the water. As I strained my eyes for a closer look, it waggled under Amaretto out of view for a few seconds before returning. It hovered there another second, and in a burst of purple light it disappeared below the surface, and I felt Pudge was with me.

"No more demons," I repeated as I adjusted Pudge's old cap on my head.

About the author

D.D. Corbitt is a former award-winning journalist, journalism adviser and American history teacher from South Florida. Corbitt graduated from Miami-Dade College (AA), University of Miami (BSC) and Nova Southeastern University (MS) She spent eight years living and traveling aboard her sailboat the *s.v. I & I* based in Tavernier, Florida. A self-proclaimed "child of the swamp," she spent her teens in the Everglades and the South Florida backwaters. An avid scuba diver, she is a former Instructor, Divemaster and holds certifications in underwater archaeology, habitat diving, wreck diving, among others. She assisted in mapping and cataloging the 1715 Spanish shipwreck the *Populo* in Biscayne National Park in the 1980s.

Corbitt is a frequent traveler to The Bahamas and several Caribbean islands.

Today she is "between boats" and divides her time between her home in Naples, Florida and the Florida Keys. She is the proud mother of one grown son and proud mentor to several former students. She shares her living space with her Irish setter, Riley and Bombay black cat, LuckyCat (who bites).

Her guilty pleasures include riding her Softail Deluxe Harley-Davidson, walking and camping in the swamp, needlepoint and stitching, reading history books and spending as much time as possible in, under and on the ocean.